Gone Bad

Also by Lesley Choyce
In the SideStreets series:
Hell's Hotel
Last Chance

Gone Bad

Lesley Choyce

James Lorimer & Company Ltd., Publishers
Toronto

James Lorimer & Company Ltd., Publishers acknowledges the support of the Ontario Arts Council. We acknowledge the financial support of the Government of Canada through the Canada Book Fund for our publishing activities. We acknowledge the support of the Canada Council for the Arts for our publishing program. We acknowledge the Government of Ontario through the Ontario Media Development Corporation's Ontario Book Initiative.

Cover Image: iStockphoto

Library and Archives Canada Cataloguing in Publication

Choyce, Lesley, 1951-
    Gone bad / Lesley Choyce.

(SideStreets)
Previously published under title: Good idea gone bad.
Issued also in electronic format.
ISBN 978-1-55277-709-1 (pbk.).—ISBN 978-1-55277-710-7 (bound)

    I. Title. II. Series: Choyce, Lesley, 1951- . Good idea gone bad.
III. Series: SideStreets

PS8555.H668G6 2011   jC813'.54   C2010-907697-4

James Lorimer &
Company Ltd., Publishers
317 Adelaide Street West,
Suite #1002
Toronto, ON, Canada
M5V 1P9
www.lorimer.ca

Distributed in the
United States by:
Orca Book Publishers
P.O. Box 468
Custer, WA USA
98240-0468

Printed and bound in Canada.
Manufactured by Webcom in Toronto,
Ontario, Canada in February, 2011.
Job # 375119

MIX
Paper from
responsible sources
FSC® C004071

Chapter 1

Let me tell you about the night we pounded that kid Jeffrey. He had it coming, so you couldn't say it was our fault or anything. At least that's the way I saw it then. People like that, I figured, shouldn't even be allowed on the streets, if you know what I mean. I didn't know much about him. I just knew he was a wannabe rapper. The worst type. A wannabe white rapper. And I hated rap and hip hop, especially by white guys doing it.

Anyway, it was one of those boring nights in Halifax, right? No action, no music, nothing happening. All we had was one bottle to share. And that had been empty for some time now. Ever since my old band broke up, I was finding it a lot harder to keep myself entertained. I mean, it used to be fine as long as I could bash — I'm a drummer, see? We played heavy music. The hardcore stuff. Not that wimpy crap. We played loud, and we played like murder. Whole neighbourhoods moved out when we practised cover tunes from Alice in Chains, The Dwarves, and Goatsnake, or even some of our own stuff. But that was all over thanks to the fact that we could never get along for more than two practices without somebody getting into a fight. It was all good fun, usually nothing more than a few stitches apiece. But the equipment kept getting wrecked and we couldn't afford repairs. So the band was dead and buried.

A drummer without a band is one lost dude. One lost dude leads to another, I guess, which is why I started hanging out again with Jordan, Eric, and Logan. They'd been my buddies from the old days when we were kids and ruled the playground. Nowadays, like me, these guys disliked boring scenes. If nothing was happening, we'd make it happen. Like this night in front of the library on Spring Garden Road.

It started out harmless enough. Logan suggested we have a contest to see who could hit the Winston Whatsisname statue with a big gob of spit from the farthest away. Mild entertainment, I admit. But it was cool because it grossed out a bunch of classy looking, uptight women who were walking by. Eric missed his shot and nearly landed a wad on the back of one of them. It splatted down on the sidewalk beside her. She turned and gave us all a look that said she thought we were disgusting. I smiled.

Well, Eric won the spitting contest but not

before he "accidentally" caught some guy in a suit with a big gob on the man's cheek. Buddy came after Eric but then backed off when he saw Big Jordan and me there too. Too bad 'cause we could have wasted him.

Like I say, it was a slow night. I had my drumsticks in my back pocket. They're good to have around for some practise. Or to shove up somebody's nose if need be. It was maybe nine o'clock at night. The moon was shining down on that great big goober that Eric had planted on Winston Whatsisname's ass from maybe two metres away.

Jordan was feeling creative so he kicked over the trash can and started to spread the contents around the lawn. Jordan is not what you call friendly to the environment.

Of course people were staring, but they were all too wimped to stand up to us. That's how we knew we were in control.

Since there was nothing much for me to do, I finished emptying the trash can, set it upside down, and got out my sticks. I got a decent enough sound going, and the boys started to join in. Logan gave it his best air guitar, his scraggly black hair hanging down over his face. Eric and Jordan launched into singing their gross-out version of "Nazis in Love."

A couple of little geeks — seventh-graders, I'd guess — stopped to watch us. We stopped playing. Logan, who I think had some kind of merit badge in hassling little kids, asked them if they had any money.

"Pick on somebody your own size," I warned him.

"Shut up, Cody," Logan snapped and then turned back to the two kids. "You just watched the show. Now you gotta pay."

The kids were starting to move away.

"Not so fast," Jordan said. Big Jordan must have looked like a UFC fighter hovering over them with his big hulk of nastiness.

The seventh-graders dug deep in their pockets and handed over a couple of bucks. Logan took the money and pushed them away.

"We let 'em off easy," he said. Logan had wanted to be a bully ever since he was a little kid, but he was always too skinny to be a serious threat. Now he was sixteen. He was still skinny. But he had a really sinister look to him that made him as scary as Jordan, who depended on size and sheer ugliness for his career.

The kids ran off down the street into the darkness. We knew they wouldn't tell a soul for fear we'd get back at them. But no harm was done. Chalk it up to education.

After that, Eric, Jordan, and Logan took a break. They were sitting on the steps of the library when this guy Jeffrey showed up. I'd seen him around before, freestyling on the streets. I was still practising drums on the trash can when he stopped and looked at us. Just what I needed. The dude actually thought he was going to rap along with what we were doing.

At first, I tried to ignore him but he just kept at it — I couldn't even make out what the hell he was saying. It was pretty annoying, let me tell you.

My buddies, however, found this entertaining.

"Lose it," Eric said, walking up behind him.

The guy tried to laugh. He didn't get it.

"Who said you could be here?" Logan asked.

By now Jordan and Eric were leaning over him and Logan was breathing down his neck. I noticed the guy had on a really cool watch. "Hey, sorry," he said finally. "I guess I'll just move on."

"Move on is right," I said. I didn't want to be seen with this guy. People might get the wrong idea. I figured I had an image to maintain.

"Not so fast." Jordan had his arms crossed against his chest and stood there like some hallway monitor from hell.

I could see that the time had come to get serious. I gave a good drum roll on the trash can. The fun was about to begin. "You know, that stuff you do on the street, it really sucks. That's not music," I told the guy. "That's bullshit."

With that, Eric knocked into the back of the guy's legs, making him topple. Jordan got in the first punch. Then Logan pulled him away and said, "Let me at him."

Logan was still getting back for all the years he'd been beat up on the schoolyard, so he hit the hardest in the most sensitive places.

By now Jeffrey was lying on the sidewalk. Like an idiot, he wasn't trying to cover his face. All we had to do was just stand there and get in some good kicks. Black army boots with steel toes are excellent weapons for this sort of street cleaning.

"Can you believe this loser?" Jordan said to me. This was my signal.

The kid was already on the ground — grounded as we would say. His face was bloody and he was hurt. He deserved it for trying to hang out with us. I knew I couldn't just stand there and do nothing. Besides, the kid had it coming. So I planted a solid kick straight into his gut and heard him let go with a choking, gurgling sound. He began spitting up blood.

We all laughed.

Somebody yelled to stop. I realized then that there were people watching us from a distance. I turned but couldn't get a fix on anything except a few shadowy figures. They must have been too scared to get any closer. I saw somebody out on Spring Garden Road waving his arms in the traffic.

Seconds later I heard the police siren. Jordan broke into a big grin. Logan looked a little worried. Eric wouldn't leave without a finale so he spit on the guy and then let out a whoop.

Eric was already breaking into a run toward Grafton Street. Jordan and Logan weren't far behind him. I gave one last look at the sorry bastard crumpled on the ground. I knew the longer I stayed, the more respect the guys would owe me. I was ready to give him one good last kick when he stuck up his arm to try to stop me.

His watch caught my eye. Yeah. I grabbed for it and ripped it off his wrist, nearly wrenching his arm out of its socket.

He tried to pull back, tried to say something but it wouldn't have mattered. It was going to be great little souvenir. I caught the look on his face — fear and pain all rolled into one. Maybe somebody else right then would have felt bad. But not me. I just smiled and ran like hell to catch up with my boys.

I had a nice little adrenalin buzz going just then. Man, I felt like I was on top of the world.

Chapter 2

I wore the watch to school the next day. Every time Jordan or one of my boys saw it, they just kind of smiled. I was feeling pretty good about myself when I ran into Kelsey, the girl of my dreams.

There is no other girl in school like Kelsey. She is like something out of my imagination: a real beauty but tough as tread on the front wheel of a Harley. She has a Zelda haircut and wears tight black jeans. And of course there is the standard labret piercing, and sometimes she even wears those nerdy but oh-so-sexy glasses. Kelsey has problems at home. She'd lived on the street for a while but then ended up back home and back in school.

I'd never really lived on the street but I had problems at home too. (Hey, who doesn't?) My father used to push around both me and my mother when I was young. He stopped doing it when I started giving him some of it back. Technically

I still lived at home, but I was hardly ever there. I'd stay out as late as I could or crash at someone else's house. I was doing okay, though.

Kelsey had a tough side but she didn't drink or do drugs. Guess that was 'cause one of her street friends went from booze to pills and then overdosed. So she keeps it pretty clean that way. But if someone pisses her off, look out. One time Mr. Lillman gave her a hard time over her opinion about having condom machines in the washrooms. Lillman thought school was no place to "promote promiscuity" — as he called it. Right in front of the class, Kelsey gave this little speech about why condoms should be available in school. She ended by calling Lillman a "prune-head."

Oh, the other thing about Kelsey is that she sings and plays keyboard. Like me, she'd lost her band. In her case, it happened when she moved out of her house. By the time she came back home, her band had found a new keyboard player as well as a new image. They'd moved into music that was way too sappy for her.

Like I was saying, I was feeling pretty good about last night so I thought I should try to make use of my luck. "Yo, Kelsey," I said. "I'm still haunted by you."

She turned to look at me from behind her locker door. Her eyes were like cold, blue fire. "Haunted?"

"You know."

"I should take this as a compliment?"

"Yeah."

"Well then, thanks." She actually smiled at me, then slammed her locker door hard and began to walk away.

"Wait, I gotta tell you about what happened last night."

"I'm listening," she said as she began walking away from me. I could tell that here was a woman worth the effort. Very cool. I'd have to really impress her if I wanted to make a play. So I cleared my throat and told her the story.

She listened with her eyes straight ahead as we walked. People parted as we made our way through the school. I was trying to make myself sound like some kind of hero for what we did. I finished my story by saying, "I think we really made a statement."

Kelsey stopped in her tracks. She looked dead at me with those gorgeous, angry eyes. "You're sick," she said. "Get out of my face." And then she disappeared into a classroom and slammed the door.

I was puzzled. What's wrong with girls these days? I asked myself. I slinked off to the stairwell and sat down underneath the first-floor stairs to wait for her class to end. I felt like a wounded animal.

When the bell rang, I was there.

"What did I do wrong?" I asked her. "The guy had it coming."

"What are you? The judge and the executioner? Who made you God?"

The girl had a way with language. Nobody could put me down the way she did. But I had to admit I admired her for that. She wasn't afraid of me. She wasn't afraid of anybody. I wouldn't give up. Turn on the charm. Change the subject, I decided.

"How is your music going? Write any new songs?"

"Music's going good. I've been jamming with Alex," she said matter-of-factly. She could tell she wasn't going to shake me off. "Yeah, I wrote a new song. It's about not fitting in."

"I can relate to that."

"I thought you couldn't stand people who don't fit in, people who are different from you."

"Yeah, well, that's different."

"Is it? Cody, how many brain cells do you figure you are operating on at any given time of the day? Five, maybe six, tops? You're a complete idiot who can't tolerate anybody who's into different music or just different from you."

"So?"

"So it's the end of discussion."

Maybe I should have taken the brain cell thing as a direct insult. But I just figured this was Kelsey's style. I was sure that deep down she really liked me. If I could only get her to spend some time with me, I knew we could make it work.

"I'll change," I said. The grin on my face must have given away my sincerity, though.

"Into what?"

"Anything you want me to be," I said, but I was giggling. "Wait. Don't walk away. Last time we talked, you promised we could do some music together some time."

"I lied."

"You can't do this to me. Look, I haven't had a band for six months. I need inspiration. You're it. When can we get together?"

"I told you, I'm working on some stuff with Alex. I don't know if I'd have time."

"Alex is a dork."

"His IQ is probably double yours."

"So what does that give him, twelve brain cells?"

She laughed. I'd finally broke through.

"Who are you using for drums?" I asked.

"We run a digital drum track. We don't need a drummer. Alex has one of the best rigs on the market."

It was the ultimate insult. "Oh man, you can't be serious!"

Kelsey could tell she'd hit a nerve. "You do have feelings."

I shrugged. What was a guy supposed to say to that?

"What's so important about a live drummer?"

"Well, music is supposed to have feeling, right?"

"Yeah."

"And a machine can't feel the music like me. When I play drums, I get involved."

"I've heard you play. You're good."

I felt like a superstar. "I know."

"But you're not modest."

"I could be if you want me to be."

I was learning about women. That last line did the trick.

"Would you be cool if I asked you over to jam with Alex and me?" Kelsey asked.

"Like ice."

"But would you be nice to Alex? He's an awesome guitar player, you know."

"I'll treat him with the highest respect," I lied. I hated guys like Alex — clean cut, good grades, student council. I didn't like the way Kelsey talked about him, but I knew I could probably make him look bad in front of her. I was talented at stuff like that. It was good that Kelsey couldn't read my mind.

"Okay. If you promise to go very easy, we'll give it a try. Today after school in the garage at my house."

"I'll be there."

"Bring your drums."

"Oh yeah. That too."

Chapter 3

What a hassle. I had to pay Blake Wayne ten bucks to haul my drum gear over to Kelsey's garage. It was the last of my cash and I was feeling sorry for myself by the time we got there. I had just dragged everything out of Blake's beater when Alex was dropped off in an Audi driven by his mommy. It made me sick realizing his family had big fat bucks and that his mom did nothing but sit around and wait to haul her little Alex to band practice. I mean, what kind of music could a loser like that play?

Alex and I were setting up in the garage, giving each other the evil eye, when Kelsey walked in.

"Let's just try to find some common ground. Okay?" she asked. "Remember I was telling you, Cody, about the tune about not fitting in? It's called 'Fool's Heart.'"

I looked her up and down. She had on shredded

pants and a tight top and I knew for sure I was in love. "I remember," I said.

"Here's the basic chord structure. Alex, give him the rhythm from the drum machine."

Alex clicked on the beat and it was pretty obvious. I got the point real quick and asked him to shut it off. "I'll see what I can do to give it a little more life," I said.

Alex scowled.

Kelsey looked at us both. "One, two, three . . ."

Well, we were off and running. I was kind of loud so Alex had to crank up his amp. Then Kelsey had to turn up. I guess before you knew it we were all competing. I couldn't hear Kelsey at all as she tried to sing but I was sure she'd be impressed with my work. I was just happy to be playing music again.

When it was over, my ears were ringing pleasantly.

"It sucked," Alex said.

"Too much drums," Kelsey said. "Got to tone it down."

Might as well ask me to live without breathing.

Then Alex started in on this lecture: "Cody, what Kelsey is trying to say is that the drums need to fit in. They need to be part of the whole rhythmic pattern. You can't just hyper-exaggerate every beat. You need to temper the rhythm."

"What planet are you from?" I asked him.

"Alex is right," Kelsey said, ganging up on me. "Listen to the whole thing once — listen to it the way Alex and I have practised it."

I tucked my sticks in my armpits and sat back. I listened.

It was tight but bland. I tried to focus on the words. Stupid stuff. Who cares if you don't fit in?

"Way too mechanical," I said when they were finished. I was staring at Alex and his drum machine.

"'Controlled' is the word," Alex tried to correct me. "We had control of the song. That's what you need in a tune if you want to make it commercial. It wasn't just noise."

Yeah right, Alex. The guy was such an idiot. I picked up my sticks and hammered the floor tom just to drown him out.

When I finished, Alex turned to Kelsey. "I can't play with somebody this uncivilized."

I smashed one of my sticks down on the snare and let it go flying into the air. "You don't know anything about music," I told him.

Alex was putting his guitar down. "This is absurd."

Kelsey was angry at both of us now. "Would you two stop acting like babies? What's wrong with you?"

"I can't get into this," Alex said. "We need a drummer, yeah. But not a Neanderthal."

That was it. I was out from behind my drums and ready to jam my other drumstick down Alex's throat and use it to tear out his windpipe. Who did he think he was?

Suddenly Kelsey was right in front of me. That cold, steely blue look in her eyes made me stop in my tracks. She walked me back to my seat and picked up the missing drumstick. Then she went over to Alex. He was packing up his guitar. She picked it up and put it back in his hands.

"We're going to try this again. I want you both to bend a little. Compromise."

The word wasn't in my vocabulary.

"It's pointless," Alex said. But he was already hitting the first chord.

Kelsey was staring past me. What else could I do? I gave her a beat. I found a pace that fit to what Alex was playing. A little too slow, maybe. A little too controlled. It made me feel like I was playing underwater. But I played. Amazingly, we stayed together through the whole thing.

"Not bad," Kelsey said afterwards.

"I didn't know a guy like that could actually play real music," Alex said.

"A guy like what?" Kelsey snapped back.

Alex went mute.

"I like the words a lot," I said. I hadn't been listening to them, but I knew Kelsey would like to hear me say it.

"Thank you. Let's try it again."

We did it again and again until it was, well . . . tight. Musical. Together. I tried a couple of little fancy things and they worked. It suddenly felt good to be playing real music with real musicians again.

Kelsey was like a drill sergeant. After we played

just the one song over and over, we jammed for a bit. Alex tried to impress me with some hot licks. I wouldn't admit it but he was pretty good. I tried to give him the beat to something much heavier, the sort of dark hardcore stuff that I liked. He gave his axe a little overdrive. It was weak by my standards but it was a start.

"I don't care what kind of music we play," Kelsey said, "as long as the song has real content . . . not just empty words."

Content? Who cares? Nobody listens to lyrics. Everyone knows that. But I wasn't stupid enough to say that out loud to Kelsey. I think all six of my brain cells were functioning just then.

By the time Alex's mom came back with the Audi, he and I had come to a kind of mutual stand-off. We had learned to put up with each other for two hours.

"I think I can talk Alex into you joining us," Kelsey said to me after he was gone.

"What do you mean?"

"We're desperate for a drummer and he knows it. I think you might work out."

Now I felt like I had been manipulated. "What was this? An audition?"

"No. Remember, you invited yourself here."

"Yeah, I guess I did. So now you want me to play this civilized stuff with you two?" I was already shaking my head.

"Yeah."

"Oh." Oh boy, was she ever persuasive. "But

it's not like what I'm used to. Too tame."

"I'll write some new tunes. I'll let you have some input."

"So sometimes I'll be able to bash . . . the way I want to?"

"Sometimes."

"Cool."

Chapter 4

I guess I didn't quite take the hint that it was time to leave. I was in no hurry to get anywhere. I had no car (no driver's licence, for that matter) to haul away my drums. I had no real interest in going home. So I was just *there,* you know. And *there* was a good place to be because Kelsey was seeming more friendly. I guess she was beginning to appreciate my finer qualities. It would have been great to have a little something to drink or a bit of weed but I knew that wasn't going to happen around there.

Her mother stuck her head out the back door. "Kelsey, dinnertime. Your father doesn't look like he's going to show up. Let's eat."

"Okay, Mom."

There was a second or two of awkward silence. The thought of food was like a light bulb inside my brain. "What's for dinner?" I asked.

"You wanna stay?"

It was a half-hearted invite but that was good enough for me. I nodded. We went in the house where I got a pretty icy welcome from Kelsey's mom.

"This is Cody," Kelsey said against some pretty stiff competition from the TV. It was like a soap opera wasteland in there. Food was steaming up on the table but Mom's eyes were glued to the pregnant woman who was crying on the tube. Mrs. Dubinski didn't even look up to acknowledge my presence.

Kelsey grabbed an extra plate and put it on the table.

"Food looks good," I announced, trying to turn on the charm and sweeten her mom up a bit.

"Cody doesn't speak in complete sentences, Mom," Kelsey said. I think she was trying to be funny. I laughed at the joke. I've got this really well-practised kind of laugh where I snort in the back of my throat. Eric calls it a killer laugh. Kelsey's mom just looked at me like I was mental.

I couldn't tell you what we ate. Something with rice, I think. I hate rice paddy chow — but I tried to put on a good face.

"Good grub," I said, but Mom was about to burst into tears just as some greaseball guy on TV came in through the door where the pregnant woman was looking at her stomach. A real groaner. The commercials came on and Mom took a bite. I like commercials. They are the only things really worth watching on TV.

"That's my favourite," I said to Kelsey, pointing to the screen where they were advertising some new movie where this robot was shooting up people with a machine gun, chopping them right in half.

"Significant content," was all Kelsey had to say. Man, conversation was tough around this place.

"Your father couldn't afford the time to eat with his family," Mrs. Dubinski announced. You could tell there were really bad vibes towards Kelsey's old man.

"He's probably pretty busy," Kelsey said.

"Not likely," her Mom shot back.

Time for me to stay out of the conversation. I shovelled rice paddy chow and tried to pretend it was good. The soaps were over and so were the commercials. Nothing on but news. Mom tried to turn it off but Kelsey caught her hand. "Leave it. I'd like to watch."

My plate was empty and I was looking around for whatever, hoping maybe for dessert or something with a little grease in it, when I see this reporter on TV. She's standing in front of the steps of the library right by the statue that we spit at all the time. There was garbage all over the place and it clicked: that was the junk I dumped out of the can so I could bang my sticks. I started to say something so Kelsey would make the connection, but she put her hand over my mouth.

"This was the scene late last night where a young man was beaten and kicked by a group of teens. It's just one of a number of recent assaults that have taken place in downtown Halifax."

The camera jumped to a shot of a guy in a hospital bed. He had a couple bruises and cuts on his face. I recognized him — he was the one we thrashed last night. I was thinking, Whoa, this is cool. We made the news.

"Why do you think you were targeted for this attack?" the reporter asked.

"I don't know," he said. "I didn't do anything to deserve this."

I was thinking, Stupid jerk. We picked on you because you are a public annoyance and deserved to get straightened out a bit. What's there to figure?

"I know him," Kelsey was saying, staring intently at the guy on the screen.

"What?" Mrs. Dubinski asked with a mouthful of food. She hadn't been paying attention.

"I know him. It's Jeffrey. He was a friend of mine when I was on the street."

"Kelsey, I don't want you talking about that in front of your friend."

The interview was ending. Jeffrey was describing how we tried to teach him a lesson. Only he didn't put it that way. Then he held up his wrist. It too was all bruised. The hand had been scraped up pretty bad. "Some guy did that to steal my watch. He yanked it right off my wrist."

I was looking at the screen and gave a thumbs-up in the air. This felt like a big moment for me. Nothing I'd ever taken part in had made it on the news before.

Mrs. Dubinski wasn't watching me. "That's disgusting," she said to the TV. "What's this city coming to?"

But Kelsey was looking at me now. She looked shocked that I was smiling. I guess I should have explained to her that the guy had it coming. How was I to know she and this guy had chummed around? Then she was staring at my wrist. I was wearing the watch.

"I don't believe this," Kelsey said, shaking her head over her plate.

"And this is an artist's rendition of what one of the attackers looked like," the reporter said. "If you know his whereabouts, you should inform Halifax City Police."

It was a pretty bad sketch that made me look a little too fat and a little too old. Nobody would recognize me from that. I was safe. What was everybody getting so upset about, anyway? Couldn't they see we were just doing a public service?

Kelsey was freaking now but she couldn't quite bring herself to say anything with her mom in the room.

"If they find the guy, they should just cut him up into little pieces and flush him down the toilet," Mrs. Dubinski said.

"I think I'll be going now," I announced. "Thanks for the chow."

I was up and moving out of there. Kelsey's mom was still rattling on about what the world was coming to and who should get what kind of cutting up. Kelsey followed me out the door and closed it behind her. Suddenly she was like a volcano.

"Get out of here, Cody!"

"What's the problem?"

"Just get out!"

Now I was mad. Here she invited me in for dinner like we were pretty tight and now suddenly she was screaming at me in her front yard. "What did I do wrong? I didn't do anything to you."

"Man, you are really dumb. You just don't get it, do you?"

"That guy deserved what he got," I suddenly snapped. I didn't like anyone trying to lecture me. "If you knew him you must have known he was a parasite."

"So you beat on him just because you didn't like him?"

"Look, you know that whole white rap thing is so fake and so lame. Sometimes you have to let those guys know what the bottom line is."

"I don't believe you. Tell me, just what is the bottom line?"

I mean she was pushing me, pushing me too hard. I didn't need a lecture from some girl. Who was she to tell me my way of thinking was wrong? She'd never understand. Man, I felt so pissed off that I wanted to bust somebody right then and there. I took off out of there before I went out of control.

I couldn't believe I let a girl make me feel so mad. I had to do something, right? Then I saw this car parked behind the store; it was all silver, a nice set of wheels, a BMW yet. So I made my statement. I picked up a good jagged rock and walked back up the alley. Then I scraped the rock across the hood, leaving a long scar in the paint. For good luck, I took it and pounded once, hard on the metal until it made a little crater and the car alarm went off.

The back door of a store opened and the guy saw me. He started yelling in some foreign language. I thought maybe he'd come after me. That would have been sweet. But he didn't. He went back in to call the cops, I guess, and I just walked away as cool as could be.

After the news, I felt like I should return to the scene of the crime, as they say, and see if anyone would recognize me from the artist's sketch the cops did. Fat chance of that, really, so I was hoping to maybe just relive a few of those fond memories of last night.

Eric was there hassling a couple of winos. I watched him from a distance before I went over to see what was up. When I saw he was joking around with the winos like they were all old friends, I didn't like it. After all, winos were just low-life scum. Better they should all be out of the way somewhere so we didn't have to look at them. I told Eric so.

"Relax, Cody," he said.

But I wasn't relaxed. Ever since Kelsey told me off, I felt like crud. Jordan and Logan showed up just about then.

"We were on the news, dudes," Logan announced.

"I was on the news," I corrected him. "It was a drawing of me they showed."

"We were all in on it," Jordan told me. "Don't try to hog the glory, Cody."

When you feel the way I was feeling then — pissed off, confused, angry — you're gonna lose your cool on someone. I guess Jordan just happened to be the one in the way. "Jordan, you're a complete and total idiot."

The two winos were looking at me now out of their bleary-eyed haze. Eric and Logan were intent on watching how Jordan was going to take it. Big, snarly Jordan was always too gross and too ugly for his own good.

"Screw you," Jordan said.

"It's just like you to try and take the credit when I'm the one who gets involved in the serious action."

"What do you want? You want this?" Jordan showed me his fist. I stared at the bony white knuckles, at the scars and the three shiny rings.

I didn't know what I wanted. I hated the way I felt just then. I had a flash of that guy in the hospital bed. I saw Kelsey's face swim up into my head. They had made me feel this way. It wasn't fair.

Jordan was breathing hard, like a fat slobbering pig. For that alone, I wanted to bust him. It would have felt good.

"I take it back," I said, not meaning a word of it. "I don't know what got into me." That part was true.

Jordan was still huffing as I walked away. "Apologize!" he demanded.

"Sorry," I said cynically, still not turning back to look at them. I threw my hands in the air. I didn't care if I ever saw those bastards again.

Chapter 5

That next day at school, I felt like Jordan and Logan were watching every move I made, everywhere I went. They had their eyes on me when Alex approached me in the cafeteria. He had on a My Chemical Romance t-shirt.

"I've decided I want you in the band," he said. It came as a real shock. "I think you add an interesting touch. I was watching some videos last night and I get it now. It looks good to have a drummer who plays it like a heavy, some guy who looks like an animal. It's an interesting image. But it will only work if you adjust to what Kelsey and I are doing."

"How do I have to adjust?"

"We've got a goal here, you know. We want to make it. We want to produce something that is commercially viable."

"Bullshit."

"Not bullshit. We can do it. Kelsey is a dynamite songwriter. She can do anything. All three of us can create the right chemistry."

"Have you talked to her about me? Are you sure she wants me in the band?"

"She said so yesterday. She was trying to convince me to accept you."

"Ask her today."

"Well, I did," Alex admitted. "I don't know. She was just kind of moody. Maybe it's her old man or something. Don't take it personally."

"How come you're on my side?"

"I like you, man," Alex said. The words were less than sincere.

"Bullshit number two."

"I'm serious. We're different but that's what'll make us unique. It's the chemistry. That's what will make us good."

"You're desperate for a drummer," I translated. "And you know I'm good."

"Okay. Have it your way. We're desperate for a drummer and it's our time to move. We've been treading water for too long, Kelsey and I."

"What about the good part."

"Okay. You're good, Cody. Whaddaya say?"

I could tell Alex would be a really good salesman some day. Or maybe something worse — a lawyer or a politician. Mostly I wanted to get something going with Kelsey. I wanted her to understand me. And I wanted to play music again. Even if it wasn't totally hardcore. Maybe I'd be able to shift some of their emo tunes in the right direction. So why not?

"I'm in," I said.

"I'll see what I can do to put Kelsey in a better mood."

Jordan and Logan couldn't understand why I was talking with Alex. Who could figure it? As I walked past them I thought I'd give them something to chew on. "He just wanted to consult me on a worry he had over school spirit. I told him we could boost morale if they served beer instead of milk."

Nobody laughed. Jordan eyed me with suspicion. Logan cracked that evil crooked smile — his trademark. I had them confused and that felt good. I also knew I had stepped one foot over the line just by talking to Alex. I was in no man's land and wondered if I could ever go back.

After school, Kelsey found me. "Come clear your drums out of my garage. I want them out of there. Today."

I thought I'd try a different approach. We'd had some harsh words. I knew better now. You have to handle women with a certain kind of psychology so they think they are winning the battles. My old man taught me that. It was probably the only reasonable word of advice he ever gave me. But then he, of course, always took things too far.

"Tell me about the street," I said, wanting to change the subject. "Tell me what it was like."

I caught her off guard. She turned her back on

me like she was going to walk away but then she wheeled round. "Jeffrey was one of the few good dependable people I knew there. He's a little odd. You're right about that. People pick on him for it. Guys like you. I've seen Jeffrey and his friends get thrashed before — just for being who they are."

"It comes with the territory," I admitted.

"Why?"

I could see I was heading down Dead-End Alley again. Big mistake. I took a deep breath and looked down at my shoes. "I wouldn't have beat on him," I said, "if I'd known he was your friend."

"Oh great," she said sarcastically. "I'll make you a list of all my friends so you won't beat on them. What about everybody else? Who you gonna grind into the dirt next?"

"I get over-excited sometimes," I tried to explain. "It's something that happens when I'm around guys like Jordan and my other friends."

"You think you impress them by beating up street performers?"

I blinked. That was exactly the way it worked but I'd never admitted it to myself. I sure wasn't about to admit it to her. "Nah. I do it 'cause I have to." I swallowed hard and tried to pretend I felt sorry about it. "But it's different now. I'm changing."

"On the street, I knew guys like you. They acted that way because they were hurting inside. Hurting bad. In that sense, they were just like me. Only I didn't have to send somebody to the hospital to make myself feel better."

She was looking at the watch again.

"If that guy was so down and out, how come he had something like this? Somebody paid big bucks for this beauty," I asked.

"Jeffrey was freestyling in front of the lineup at the Palace one night. This guy came along. Turned out to be Vin Grecko from the band Crime Therapy. He was in town for a concert. Vin liked the way Jeffrey performed. He gave him the watch. It blew us all away."

"Too much." I looked at the watch on my wrist and thought it was pretty cool that it had once belonged to Vin Grecko.

"Jeffrey thought it was a good omen."

"What do you mean?"

"Like good luck. He wants to make it as a hip hop artist."

"Fat chance he has hanging out on street corners."

"Some people don't have many options."

"What about you? You had options. You went back home. How come?"

"Home sucks. My mother and father argue a lot when my father comes home . . . which isn't often. The rest of the time, my mom watches soaps and tells me how messed up her life is. I thought my life was too, until I lived on the street. That was worse."

"I get the picture."

"I didn't miss much about home except for the fact that it wasn't quite as dangerous as the street.

And the music. I didn't have my keyboard. I wasn't writing songs. I felt really lost."

"I felt the same way when my band busted up. Lost."

"Alex wants you with us."

"I know. But you don't."

"I did."

"Before you found out about the thing in front of the library."

"Yeah."

"Maybe I'll grow out of it. That's what my mother says."

"You mean you're admitting that what you did was wrong?"

This was getting tricky. Kelsey was looking for a big time confession. "I'm not always right, I guess."

Her eyes opened wide. "I don't believe I'm hearing this."

"Well, I want to be in your band. I like that song of yours. I liked the words. They made sense."

"I thought content didn't matter. 'Nobody listens to words,'" she said, as if she had read my mind.

"That's what I mean. I was wrong. I listened. You were singing about what it feels like to always be on the outside. How it hurts. I know that feeling. I've been on the outside a lot." I wanted to go on and tell her about the line that had just been drawn between me and the guys but I figured I had already said too much.

"You'd be nothing but trouble if you were in our band."

I smiled and shook my head. "I'll try to be good," I said. I suddenly felt like a little boy making a promise. And for a split second, looking at Kelsey, I almost thought I was telling the truth. I'd do just about anything to be around her.

* * *

Session number two in Kelsey's garage was a wild success. I tried real hard to be good, to be co-operative, and it paid off. I picked up quickly on about three of the tunes Kelsey had written. They were dark. It wasn't exactly my style but I was getting the feel of it. The music felt good. The drums beneath my sticks felt like they were working on their own. Alex was beaming like a little kid as he picked through a series of serious licks with his distortion pedal to the limit. I bet you could hear us five blocks away at the Canadian Tire store.

"Okay, let's try this," Kelsey said. "You know how they used to do protest songs in the old days?"

"Ah, c'mon," I groaned. "I'll do anything but folk music. Don't go sixties on me."

"No way. No sixties. This is now. But it is a protest song."

"What's the issue?" Alex asked.

"Condoms."

Alex looked puzzled.

"Alex, you know how the school board muzzled

41

the student council for wanting to have condom machines installed in the school washrooms."

"We voted in favour of it. We just couldn't make them do it. They argued that kids shouldn't be having sex and that putting the machines in the school would be promoting . . . what was the word . . . promiscuity."

"So?" I asked. "What's wrong with promiscuity?"

"So I wrote this. You'll love it, Cody. It's very angry, very loud. Play as loud as you want."

She ran through it once so I could hear the lyrics and she explained the chords to Alex.

"Don't you think it's just too limited in its appeal?" Alex asked. He didn't seem that keen on the song. "We should be thinking about a broader audience. This is just about a measly little school issue."

"But it's a real issue, Alex. I need to write songs about real issues. Things that matter."

"Content, man," I told Alex. "Kelsey wants the words to mean something." I would be on her side for this one. I still didn't care what she sang, as long as she sang it loud and sang it with punch. Condoms or condominiums, who cares?

Alex gave up. "Is that an F after the A minor on the bridge?" he asked Kelsey.

"D first, then A minor."

"Got it."

Three weak tries and then on the fourth time I found the right beat, hammered on the floor tom for the bridge, and then piled on the wood for the end. Kelsey was beaming. My ears were ringing. Music was making me deaf.

"We need a name for the band," Alex said when the song ended. "We need something that fits."

It was some kind of commitment that we were in fact a band, not just a trio of losers making noise in a garage.

"Good idea," said Kelsey. Another commitment. "But it can't sound too wimpy."

"I got it," I said. "Scream Static." That was the name I had kicking around in my head for weeks now.

The name stuck like peanut butter to the roof of your mouth.

Chapter 6

For a couple of weeks, music took over my life. We put in long hours practising in Kelsey's garage. We recorded some of our stuff with a program on her computer and it sounded pretty solid.

I only ever saw her father once. He came home early from work one day and started yelling at Kelsey.

"How come I can't park my car in my own garage?" he demanded.

"We're practising," Kelsey said. "We need the space. Who cares if your car sits outside?"

"I care," he said. "It's my garage." The guy looked like some kind of angry rooster.

I thought I could help out in the argument so I walked over.

"What is this?" dear old dad asked his little girl.

"This is my friend, Cody," she said.

I held out my hand but the dude just shook his

head and walked off towards the house.

"I think you scared him," Alex said.

"I was just trying to be friendly."

Kelsey's mom had begun to like me okay. I offered to take the trash out and stuff like that. So I thought I could also impress her old man into seeing that I was okay. Guess it didn't work.

"Don't mind him," Kelsey said. "He was born with a bad temper."

A few minutes later I could hear him inside the house arguing with Kelsey's mom.

"We better get back to work and make some noise to drown out the lovebirds so the neighbours won't hear," Kelsey said.

Thanks to my drumming, the music was starting to have some real muscle. We mostly did original material that Kelsey wrote, like "The Condom Song." And it was her songs that made life pretty interesting for SS.

Word reached us that the school was going to have a dance. A couple of the teachers, Mr. Alphonse and Mrs. James, were holding auditions to select a band, instead of hiring a stupid DJ for once.

"No way," I said. "They'll never hire us in a million years."

"We should give it a shot," Alex insisted. "Look, if we get the gig, it would be the first time kids from this school play live music for a dance."

"Oh yeah, right. Just as long as no one listens to our lyrics," Kelsey said.

"So we don't play anything to offend them,

that's all," Alex responded.

Kelsey gave him a foul look.

"Mr. Alphonse likes me," Alex said. "I'm getting an A in his class."

I slammed the high hat with my sticks. "Look, like I said, we won't get hired. They ain't gonna hire us. Let's just forget it."

Alex went bug-eyed and I felt like belting him just for being such a douche.

"I say we try out anyway," Kelsey said. "What's wrong with that?"

"Just no controversial songs, right?" Alex said. "And no heavy bashing. We keep it real tight and real clean."

I dropped my sticks and held my hands in front of my face like I was about to pray. "I promise not to play anything I wouldn't play in church," I said.

Out of the corner of my eye, I saw Kelsey smile. I think my charm was starting to get through to her.

We learned a couple of cover tunes of stuff you'd hear on the radio. I went along for the ride. The two bands before us were older — guys in college, I think. The first band did old songs that made me want to throw up. All clean-looking dinks in ties and polished shoes. My guess is they had been locked up in a time capsule and were just released after thirty years underground.

The next group had a guy on a turntable and two wannabe rappers trying to look hard-ass and inner city. I had to leave the room until they were through.

One other band failed to show, so that left us. Alphonse and James went out for coffee while we set up. About twenty kids had heard the music and sneaked into the gym. It was dark at the back and when the teachers returned, they didn't notice that we now had an audience. I felt a lot better about having some real humans in the room, instead of just teachers. I tightened down my drums. Alex and Kelsey got in tune and we were ready.

We were very tame through two songs. I knew we were doing okay because Alphonse hadn't told us to quit. We had one more tune to do. Alex said we should do our last song — "Waiting out the Dawn." Real middle-of-the-road monotony, as far as I was concerned.

But, hey, you can only keep a pound of dynamite in a closet for so long before someone gives it a match. And I looked way in the back of the gym and saw some of the kids starting to leave. We weren't impressing anyone.

I looked at Kelsey. "We do 'The Condom Song,'" I said.

"No," she said. "Let's stick to the plan."

"Don't blow it now," Alex whispered to me, and hit the first chord to "Waiting."

I nodded to the back of the room. Kelsey saw the kids leaving. A couple of her friends were back there, I think, because now she saw what had become of us — a trio of wimped-out, gutless musicians on the road to Muzak. We had to act quickly if we didn't want to lose our audience or even our reputation (before we even had one).

"One, two, three," I counted off and then — slam. I did the drum intro, setting up the backbeat for "The Condom Song." Very original. Very loud. And full of meaningful lyrics. Alex had no choice but to go along since the song was already rolling.

The kids stopped dead in their tracks. Alphonse and James looked up from their coffees and stared at us like we had all just changed into werewolves before their very eyes. Kelsey belted out the words loud and clear:

When there's problems that you just can't hide,
Don't cover it up, that's suicide.
No head in the sand, got to make a stand;
It's just a condom machine, not a lie routine —
Put your fears aside, let the kids decide,
let the people decide,
let us all decide.

Well, maybe there was some language even stronger than that. But to Kelsey, these were the words that mattered. The song had so much pounding energy and anger that you could feel it in the air when we hit the final note. The kids in the back of the gym started to cheer. Alphonse turned around and shouted at them.

"You are not supposed to be in here. This is a closed session. Now leave immediately or I'll take down your names."

I had a sudden craving to zero in on the back of

his head while he was turned around and launch a big gob of spit straight at his bald spot. But I was trying to be good — for Kelsey and for the band. Besides, I wasn't as skilled as, say, Eric who could have picked off a sparrow flying across the yard.

Instead, I sat quietly, waiting. Waiting for what? For somebody to say something, I guess.

Alex was mad, yes, but he was trying to be cool. "Now we wouldn't be playing that song at the dance, Mr. Alphonse. We just want to let you see that we have range in our music. We're very versatile."

"I'm sure you are, Alex," Mrs. James interjected. "But we feel that the, um, style of your music is a bit too . . . volatile for a school dance."

Volatile? What the hell was that supposed to mean? I didn't know if I had just been insulted or what.

"What Mrs. James is trying to say," Alphonse kicked in, "is that we couldn't tolerate anything that loud. Or that provocative. It would, after all, be a school-sponsored function."

I gripped onto my sticks and felt the drops of sweat forming in my armpits. School-sponsored function? I'd like to show him a school-sponsored function.

"What is it you are trying to say, Mr. Alphonse?" I asked.

Alphonse sighed. "I really am impressed by your range, as Alex calls it. I just don't think anyone could dance to your music. The beat is all wrong. I just think you might cause too many problems."

In other words, we didn't get the job.

"You don't like us because we're too original," Kelsey shot back at him through her mic. The words echoed in the gym.

"We don't need to justify our decision," Mrs. James said softly.

The kids were still in the back of the room. No one had left. Somebody back there in the darkness was giving us a thumbs-up.

We had just been rejected and I was mad. When I felt like that, I was used to busting something, but this was school and I was in dangerous territory. I started to bash away on my drums — just some hard, brutal sounds, rolls on the floor tom, heavy pounding on the snare. A couple of kids clapped but Alphonse and James were in the back of the room now shuttling them all away. And then they too were gone. We were alone in the empty gym.

Chapter 7

Alex was real upset about the way things went. I guess it would have been a big deal for him to have a chance to play at a dance in front of all his snobby friends. I could never figure the guy out. He wouldn't come out and say anything to Kelsey but he put the blame on me. "You blew it, Cody. It was all your fault."

Big freaking deal. We had made our point, didn't we? I figured I could get back at both Alphonse and James by simply doing some damage to their cars in the school parking lot. All my time hanging out with Jordan, Eric, and Logan was not a waste. The boys had taught me life skills — tire slashing, gas tank modification, and even engine damage. It was just a matter of selecting the right tactic to fit the crime.

I tried to explain this to Kelsey. I was sure she'd understand. We'd been muzzled. Our music, her song, would not be heard by the student body.

"Cody, you think in very crude terms."

"Thank you."

"It wasn't a compliment."

"It sounded like one, coming from you. You always have such a sweet way of saying things."

"Stop calling me sweet."

"Oh, sorry. I forget you've been brainwashed. Girls aren't supposed to be sweet anymore."

"Forget sweet. Try sophisticated."

"You want to help me roll their cars into the harbour?"

"Grow up. Let me explain sophisticated." And she did.

In truth, the plan she outlined lacked the sting of action that involved serious physical damage but I was willing to go along with anything Kelsey wanted out of me. She had me twisted around her finger like a pretzel, as the saying goes.

We knew Alex would never go along with her idea and decided ahead of time that we'd take the rap for it. We wouldn't let him get punished.

The next morning I met Kelsey outside her house and she had the memory stick with the MP3 file of "The Condom Song" that we'd recorded. We hovered around outside the school until everybody was cozy and comfy in their homerooms. As you might have guessed, it was the one and only Alex who had the job of doing the morning PA. He was reading the announcements and trying to sound like a professional.

When the coast was clear, Kelsey and I crawled beneath the hallway windows of the office and threw open the door to the school radio station booth. Alex swivelled round as we burst into the room.

"What the —"

But it was our time, not his. I put my hand over his mouth and yanked his chair backwards. He struggled so I had to wrestle him out the chair and yank his arm up behind him.

"Not so rough," Kelsey scolded me. But I liked being rough. Despite the fact that we had been playing music together, I never fully trusted Alex. He always thought he was too good. I loved putting douches like him in his place.

Kelsey looked at the control board. She popped in the stick with our tune. She cranked up the volume and suddenly every homeroom in the school was getting a taste of Scream Static at our best.

I let go of Alex and barricaded myself against the door at the onslaught of the secretaries, the principal, and Mr. Locksley, the guidance counsellor, but when Mr. Gideon, the wrestling coach, showed up, I was overpowered. The door opened. "The Condom Song'' was cancelled and we were all in very deep shit.

One verse and one chorus had made it out of the little booth, though, and into the hearts and minds of the students at our school.

I think I really hurt Alex. Something I did to his shoulder. Not my fault, really. I was used to fighting guys who could fight back, not little boys who get driven around in their mommy's Audis.

It was the VP, Mr. Alphonse, who sat us down (with Coach Gideon in the room for backup, I might add) to read us the riot act. Detention all around. Definite suspension if we tried to stir up any more trouble with the condom machine issue. "It's a dead issue," he said. "You have acted way beyond the bounds of reason. Alex, I'm most disappointed in you for being involved."

Alex was rubbing his shoulder.

"Alex wasn't involved," Kelsey said.

"I find it hard to believe you weren't all involved," Alphonse said.

Alex could have bailed just then, but he didn't. He said nothing. For the second time since I'd known him, I think I really liked the guy.

The price you pay for fame. In our case, I think the detentions were worth it. People in the halls were talking about the song. They were talking about SS as well. They were saying it was a crime we didn't get the gig playing at the dance. Kelsey had posted the tune everywhere on the Internet and almost everyone had downloaded their own version. I got a nice little glow walking the halls watching kids mouthing the words to Kelsey's song as they went from class to class.

Then one day I was sitting in English trying to get my rest when Mrs. Lyons directed a question at Kelsey. We were supposed to be studying *The Mountain and the Valley* by some dude named Buckler. Mrs. Lyons said that the book had been banned in some schools. The class was in the middle of a discussion on censorship.

"Why do you think *The Mountain and the Valley* would be banned from schools?" she asked Kelsey.

Kelsey didn't like being called on in class, I knew. She had a rep for being a kid who'd once lived on the street, who'd been in trouble. Nobody thought she was very smart but I knew better. "I think it's a lot like my song," she said.

Suddenly, everyone in the class was alert. "How do you mean that?" Mrs. Lyons asked.

"Well, I think people — adults, at least — are afraid of my song because it tells the truth. They feel threatened because they'd rather not have to deal with the difficult issues — things like sex and STDs and AIDS."

I was ready for Lyons to shoot her down, tell her that she was changing the subject or something so I jumped to my feet. "We've got a right to express the way we feel about things. Kelsey's got a right. We all do. People are going to listen to our song. They're already listening and you can't stop them."

Instead of giving me a hard time, Lyons actually looked pleased. "Good point, Cody. It's good to hear you voicing your opinion in class."

Well, that was a bit of a shock. I sat down, feeling a little dizzy. This was weird beyond belief. I was wondering what was coming over me. Here I was getting involved in some geeked-out classroom discussion and the teacher was actually agreeing with me. Was I losing it or what?

Some other guy raised his hand. He said that just because a song was controversial it didn't mean it was good, and that the school made the right decision by keeping out condom machines and by yanking our song off the PA.

I could have wiped up the parking lot with him and his opinions. I was ready to tell him so in front of the class. Who the hell did he think he was to try and keep Kelsey's song from being heard?

But then this other freaky thing happened. The Chinese kid who called himself Paul had his hand up. Lyons called on him. I couldn't stand his face and thought it was a big mistake that we had even allowed his family into the country, let alone allowing him into the school. Now he was going to throw in his two cents about censorship. He couldn't speak English worth spit.

"Before we left China, my parents got put in jail because of what they said in the newspaper. When they did it a second time, we had to leave the country or they would have gone to prison. Like Cody, I think everyone should be free to speak."

The bell rang. Class was over. I found myself staring at Paul, wondering how it could be that this skinny Asian kid had come to my defence in an argument in English class. It made my skin crawl just to think that we shared something in common at all. I was beginning to wonder just what the world was coming to.

Chapter 8

I think that was the beginning of the legend. Even Alex had to admit the controversy was good, although I do think he never forgave me for being so heavy-handed on him in his little radio studio.

Kelsey's old man had given up the idea of ever parking his car back in his garage because it had become permanent SS headquarters. I don't even know why we practised so much or so hard. We just did. The music drove us to it. And every time I turned around, Kelsey had a new song she wanted us to try. It seemed like she had a new song for every opinion she had. And the girl had some strong opinions.

Sometimes kids would show up to watch. Like — believe it — we were getting a following. The band that played at the school dance was a big flop. Somebody had tried to sneak a copy of "The Condom Song" onto the sound system, only to get it squelched. This led to some shouts of "Censorship!" but, of course, I wasn't there to see it. You wouldn't catch me at a high school dance.

Although I have to admit these days I wasn't doing much other than the band. There was a bit of chill between me and my old boys. I guess they were thinking I was a bit of a snot for spending so much time with the band, but this was my life now. They must have been curious though, once they started to hear about our reputation. And that's why they showed up at Kelsey's garage.

We were working on some new material that was really kicking. I looked up from my drums to see ugly old Jordan staring back at me. "You're not as good as you used to be," he said. Eric and Logan just grinned.

I knew what he meant. He meant I was too controlled, not outrageous enough. I guess I had mellowed a little, it was true.

I didn't know what to say to them but they were giving Alex the creeps. Alex said he was going to split early. He didn't say why but the reason was obvious. He went inside to call home for a ride. When his mom pulled in the driveway, she saw Jordan and the boys lounging right there alongside the leaked oil from the Dubinski family car. Alex's mom didn't look too happy to see the quality of our home-grown audience.

Eric started making crude remarks about Alex's mother and I had to tell him to shut it. Once Alex was packed up and gone, Jordan cornered me and said he was "very disappointed" in how I turned out.

"What is that supposed to mean?" I asked.

He looked at Kelsey. "She a lesbian?" he asked me. Jordan had a problem with any girl who didn't know how to "stay in her place." He lumped them all together as lesbians. And he hated lesbians.

"I don't label myself anything," Kelsey told him, not waiting for me to answer.

"Yeah," I said, reinforcing the point.

Logan laughed. "She's got you whipped, Cody."

What could I say to them? Eric was leering at Kelsey now. They were all trying to get me going so I'd do something stupid. But maybe Kelsey had influenced me. I wasn't going to let them get to me.

"We miss you on the street, man," Jordan said. "We didn't expect to see you waste your time on this music thing. It's not like your old band. You used to be hardcore. This is too lame."

"We're good," I said. "You heard what happened at school?"

"It was cute, but we weren't impressed," Eric said. "If the song had any real impact, it would have made everybody crazy. The whole school would have been trashed."

"Just 'cause kids didn't go wild and destroy the school, you don't think the song meant anything?" Kelsey asked.

Logan snorted. "Oh, it meant something, all right. It meant that Cody here sold us out."

"What? How did I sell you out?"

"The music, man. The street. The stuff we believe in." Jordan was angrier now and shoving a fist at my face.

In their minds I had crossed a line, turned my back on them. I was a traitor. There was a rift between us and it was getting wider. What was it we had believed in, anyway? We believed in having fun. We believed in cleaning the junk off the streets — the human trash. We believed in making up our own rules.

No. We believed in nothing.

But I hadn't really changed. Not much. I still didn't believe in anything other than what was good for me. The only difference was I had decided that the music was good for me. Kelsey and the music. I wasn't about to turn my back on those two things to get back in with these guys.

"Get out of here," I told Jordan. "Go find some little kid to beat up on."

Jordan never took my advice well. He hadn't changed. He picked up a crowbar from a corner of the garage and was walking towards me when a car pulled up in the driveway. I guess he figured it was Kelsey's old man or something. Or maybe he only wanted to make the threat. If he was gonna thrash me, he'd do it some time when I wasn't ready, some place where nobody but his boys would see. He'd catch up to me on a dark street and do it. Now he had a girl and maybe her father watching. Jordan didn't like wiping out anybody unless he was sure he could get away with it.

I didn't blink. Jordan threw the crowbar through the front of my bass drum, ripping the front skin. Then he, Logan, and Eric left.

It turned out it wasn't Kelsey's father at all but some guy in a beat-up Volvo. As he tried to get out of the car, Jordan was walking past and shoved the door back at him angrily, chomping the poor dude's leg.

I studied the damage to the front of my bass drum. No big deal, I said to myself. A lot of drummers play without a front skin on it. Now mine had a big gash with a crowbar sticking out. I decided I liked the image. Forget about being ticked-off at Jordan. I'd go with the new look.

The guy who just pulled up seemed pretty confused as he walked towards us. "Friends of yours?" he asked Kelsey and me.

"We were just throwing them off the property," Kelsey said.

"I thought maybe they were part of the fan club." The guy smiled now and looked around the garage. "You're missing somebody, right?"

"Yah," I said. "What business is it of yours?"

"Oh, sorry," he said, sticking out his hand for me to shake. "I'm Barry Goddard." He handed me a little business card that said, "Barry Goddard, Independent Producer."

"Am I supposed to be impressed?"

"No, not at all."

"Then what?" Kelsey asked him.

"I heard about you guys. A kid from your school

let me hear your song, the condom thing. They even have a nickname for you. What was it . . . the Rubber Band?"

I groaned. "Spare me."

"Sorry. Look, I liked the tune. I liked the sound. Can I hear more?"

"As you can see, we're missing a guitar. It'd sound pretty empty without Alex."

"Yeah, right. But it's really the songs I'm interested in. Who does the writing?"

I pointed to Kelsey.

"You got others?"

"Yeah, lots."

"Play something, okay? Just the two of you. I'll imagine the guitar in my head."

Hey, I didn't care. I'd play music for the Pope if he asked. We did a version of "Downtown Dangerous" and "Me, You, and the Other Poor Slob." Kelsey's lyrics were getting more edge to them. She was getting more daring and I liked that. My guess was that we were moving farther out on the fringe from the really safe emo stuff. Maybe it was my positive influence. Of course, Alex was getting antsy about the direction. He kept saying we could never "go commercial" with stuff like that. But here we were with some independent producer — very small time, no doubt, but he was interested in us.

"I've got a digital recording studio in my basement," Barry said when we were done. "I'd like to record all of you sometime and see what it sounds like."

Kelsey was skeptical. "How much is it gonna cost us?"

"Nada," Barry said. "Nothing. I'd just like you guys to see what a real engineered mixed version sounds like. You're good. Kids are talking."

"What's in it for you?" I asked.

Barry threw his hands up in the air. "Who knows?"

Chapter 9

"We shouldn't get involved with small-time operators like that," Alex said, as soon as we told him about Barry.

"What could it hurt?" Kelsey answered. "We haven't exactly signed any deals. He just offered to record our stuff. At least we might end up with a good demo."

"What was he driving?" Alex asked.

"A Volvo," Kelsey said. She didn't tell Alex that it looked like a Volvo that had been driven through the streets of Baghdad during the Gulf War.

"I still think we should polish our material and hold off for a while."

"Let's just do it," I said. I was getting pretty sick of people who had to discuss everything before they acted.

"Kids are asking to hear more of our songs, Alex," Kelsey said. "If we could get some good tracks down maybe we could even burn some CDs to sell at our gigs."

I guess the idea of making a few bucks from our music appealed to Alex. He gave in.

The session was weird but cool. It wasn't exactly a basement studio. Barry lived in the basement of an old apartment building. He had a couple of dogs in there that he'd taken off the street. They sniffed me pretty seriously as I walked in. The place was a real dump. You should have caught the look on Alex's face. But after making friends with the dogs (I got down on the floor and sniffed them), I decided I liked this guy.

He did have a fairly sophisticated digital recording setup but we had to spread out all over his ratty little apartment to get arranged. Kelsey ended up in the kitchen with her keyboard. Through the mic she said, "Barry, why does the only woman here have to get stuck in the kitchen? Isn't this just a little bit sexist?" He got the joke. She had to explain to me later the thing about putting the only woman in the kitchen. So maybe it was funny, I don't know.

Alex ended up in the bedroom with his guitar and both mangy dogs, who seemed to thrive on the sound of an electric six-string.

Wouldn't you know it? I had to set up in the bathroom and keep the door closed. "Otherwise, you'll be too loud, Cody. If I want to mix this properly, I need to have you all isolated from each other."

Talk about weird. We were a band trying to play

without seeing each other. The headphones helped but it was hard playing without being able to watch Alex or Kelsey. I swore it was the last gig I'd ever do in somebody's bathroom.

We recorded "The Condom Song" and "Downtown Dangerous," Kelsey's song about her days living on the street. We played it together and then one at a time while listening to the other tracks already recorded. I was thinking it was all a waste of time, a big joke. Barry was just a hack amateur who had been bullshitting us.

But then we heard the mix. It sounded very good. In fact, it sounded too good. "That's us?" I asked.

"Scream Static just got a little bit better," Barry said.

Barry invested some money into promoting the band online. Alex didn't trust him, but that was Alex. We hadn't signed any contracts. But I thought Barry was okay. Maybe he'd help us get our sound out there.

Then CKDU, the Dalhousie University station, started playing "The Condom Song." People all over Halifax and Dartmouth were hearing it. Alex couldn't deny that we were getting attention. I could handle the glory. Clearly, if CKDU was giving us airtime, we were cutting edge.

In fact, a guy from CKDU called up Kelsey and invited us all in for a live interview. Now, it wasn't exactly MTV or anything but it seemed like a step up. Even Alex was impressed.

So we went down to Dal and I had on my shredded pants and studded belt. I had on a chopped off
t-shirt with a picture of Hitler on it. It was short
enough to let my gut hang out a little and there
were no sleeves so my armpit hairs stuck out.
Some rockers probably take years to achieve this
look, but for me it comes naturally. I am just lucky
that way. Alex had on these John Lennon type
shades and Kelsey looked . . . well, just hot. Even
university kids were looking at us like we must
be important as we walked into the Student Union
Building. The only thing missing was the stretch
limo, but I knew that pretty soon we'd be getting
driven around in something better than Barry's old
rust hulk.

So we went into the studio and I nearly freaked.
There was Jeffrey working the sound board. He
and Kelsey hugged and I wanted to gag. Maybe
now was my chance to finish the job on his face
with my boot.

"You go to school here?" Kelsey asked him.

"No, I just volunteer at the station," he answered. They were still hugging.

"It is great to see you," Jeffrey told her. But then
he saw me standing there.

What was I gonna do?

I'm sure he had never realized that the drummer of Scream Static was the guy who wasted him,
the one he described to the cops. He looked at me
and I saw fear creep into his face. Then he looked
at my watch — well, his watch. Yeah, I was still

wearing it. It had brought me good luck. But as he was looking at it, I turned my hand into a fist and silently thrust it in the air. I'd kill him if he messed up this scene for us. But I also knew that he had me. If he wanted to call the cops and have me arrested, he could do it.

I tried to get eye contact. I wanted him to know I meant business. Blab on me, little brother, and you'll soon regret it. But he looked away. "Time to get you guys on-air," he said to Kelsey and opened the door to the studio.

The interview went okay. I didn't say much. Kelsey sounded tough and sharp. Alex came off like the mommy's boy he is. All I got to say was that I learned everything I knew about drumming from playing drums since I was about twelve. The truth is, I was sweating it because I was there in this little room with no place to run if Jeffrey wanted to call the law on me. I could feel a dribble of sweat sneak out and trickle down from my armpit hairs. It made me really angry that a little worthless piece of nothing could get me worried like this.

On the way out, I was relieved to see Jeffrey was gone. I reckoned my silent threat was enough for a wimp like that to not take chances with getting me in trouble. I was doing okay after all.

Things only got better after that. During lunch at school, a couple of kids let me know they loved our tunes. Someone even tried to play a song of ours with the other lame music on the sound system in the cafeteria. But it was quickly cut off.

Alex tried to protest this to the school principal but it didn't do any good, of course. And even the local newspaper had a story about our tune being censored in the school.

Kelsey and I thought the publicity for the band was pretty decent. The paper said "The Condom Song" had "brought back to life the dead issue of installing condom machines in the school washrooms." But some parents were "offended and deeply disturbed by the language on the two songs." Alex was quoted as saying that the music was an expression of "freedom of speech." Mr. Alphonse had made the case to the press that it was "the music itself that had turned out to be such a bad influence on what was once one of the top students in the school." This was a reference to our boy Alex, just so you don't get confused. Not me.

It was all just fine with me. I could handle the hassles from any old bat or bean counter who wanted to call us names. Trouble was what I liked. Trouble was my middle name. Kelsey didn't seem to mind it, either. She was getting tougher by the minute. "People do listen to the words," she insisted.

Meanwhile, Alex had to put up with his mother and father telling him that his fellow band members were flushing his life down the crapper. He was having second thoughts about being in the band.

Kelsey and I never saw it coming at all. I guess his parents had really done a number on the guy.

He was looking down at the floor when he told us. The words hit us like a hammer to the skull. "I'm thinking of quitting," he told us. "It's costing me too much."

Chapter 10

But Alex didn't quit. He knew we had too much going for us. He missed a couple of practices and by then it was too late for him to make us change our minds about Barry. Kelsey and I both liked the guy. We all had this in common: we lived for the music. What came out of the recording sessions in the basement was nothing short of a miracle. Barry knew we were ready for a live audience. We were flying high when he announced, "I've got a job for you."

Barry had managed a couple of bar bands before. I figured he must have lied about our ages and got us a booking at a tavern or something. "We get free beer with it?" I asked.

"No. No free beer. Sorry about that, Cody. It's not that sort of gig."

"We'll settle for juice and cookies," Kelsey said. "What is it?"

"I rented a hall. We'll promote it on CKDU, put posters up all over town. I think we can pack the joint."

"How much we gonna make?"

"Depends on how many people come through the door. First we pay off the rental, then you guys get all but ten percent. Agreed?"

It sounded okay to me.

"What if nobody shows?" Kelsey asked.

"Then I lose my shirt," Barry said, "and you hoodlums get a great place to practise for the night."

The night of the gig, the place was packed, jammed tight with all kinds of people. I'd never been so nervous in all my life. We were set up, ready to blast the place. Barry had even rented a dynamite sound system that he was monitoring. It was like big time.

It was a really weird mix of people — street kids, straight kids from school, Black kids from here in the North End . . . and then I spotted my thug friends, Eric, Jordan, and Logan. What were they doing here? Unfortunately, I could guess the answer.

We started off with "The Condom Song." That got everybody revved up because it was what had established our rep. Then we peeled off into a couple of Kelsey's other tunes and I was working away at the drums, feeling like I had just become a superstar. We had all come back together with the music, despite recent differences. That was the way our band was. We fought. We argued. We disagreed. And then when it came down to the music, we worked at it until we were right on the money. Tonight we were like gold.

But, like my old man used to say, "You go flying too high with the birds and you're gonna crash." The night was going too good.

I noticed Jordan had more than just Logan and Eric along. He had scraped up some other dregs to join him. They were hanging around the back of the hall like the scum line after you drain the bathtub. Our music was loud so we could drown out their insults, but between songs Jordan and his boys were shouting some really nasty stuff. It was mostly directed at Kelsey — you know, the kind of stuff guys say. Kelsey was trying to ignore it but I knew that wasn't her style. She looked at Alex and said the name of the song I hoped she wouldn't under the circumstances.

Too late. Alex was already launched into the wailing guitar lead of "Downtown Dangerous." I had no choice but to pick up the beat and get into it. "I want to dedicate this one to the boys in the back," Kelsey said. Bad news. Whatever happened to the old days when women knew when to keep their mouths shut? I tried playing so loud that maybe no one would hear the lyrics, but tonight Kelsey had volume. Barry had already cranked up the vocals so even I couldn't whack hard enough on the drum kit to drown her out.

Kelsey was looking straight at the boys when she sang the lines:

Problems on the street are the people you meet,
animals, cannibals, racists, and creeps,
so stupid and weak they can barely speak
so they beat up on us, they'll pick anyone,
then hide in the dark or they chicken and run.

That was Kelsey. Never knew when to keep her opinions to herself. I'd heard the lyrics over and over. I knew where I fit into it but I figured it was only a song. It didn't mean anything. Just a bunch of words. And I liked the way the tune went. I had a great little drum solo near the tail end of it. But now, I guess, this song about the street had gone political.

I looked out into the crowd. Maybe we could just keep the instrumental part of the song going for like a really long time, maybe seven hours. Eventually everybody would just go home. Nothing would happen. Unfortunately, I saw more people coming into the room now. Some of Alex's buddies from school — real clean-cut front-row types. I saw some really fine looking babes come in too. And then, haunting me like a ghost — Jeffrey. Couldn't the guy take a hint?

The song ended. Alex leaned my way and said, "I'm gonna take a real quick break. I'll be right back."

Before I could say anything, he was off the stage, heading towards the door to meet his friends, Danny and Craig. I guess he was going to have them come up front or something because they had never come to hear us practise. This was a big deal that some of Alex's buds had arrived. But it was mighty bad timing.

Kelsey's words had thrown Jordan's maniac lever into high gear. He and his buddies saw Alex coming. To Jordan, Alex and his friends were a bunch of emo whiners. That's just the way his mind worked. So Jordan figured it was a great time to move in. The goons followed. In a matter of seconds, Alex, Danny, and Craig were surrounded.

Eric quickly knocked Danny to the floor and yanked off his jacket. Jordan was calling him names. Logan tripped Alex and Craig looked for an exit, but one of Eric's friends shoved him back into this little arena. This was their game and they knew how to play it well. I knew what they were trying to do. They were trying to wreck our big event. Man, I wasn't going to get down there and get involved. Whatever happened, I knew that I'd end up losing so I stayed put.

Barry was trying to get at the centre of things. All the kids had circled around but nobody really knew what was going on. Then I saw Jordan about to punch Alex in the face only to have his fist grabbed by Jeffrey. Oh my god, this was going to be ugly. If it wasn't for the fact that it was ruining the music, I would have loved this scene. I had a great seat up on stage. I could see everything. But tonight was different.

Before Jordan could get a good hold on Jeffrey, Kelsey was off the stage like a bolt of lightning and barging into the middle of things. She drove a fist into Jordan's crotch and told him to let go of Alex. "Get out of here. All of you!" she shouted.

I think Jordan actually felt the punch because he let go of Jeffrey and stood there staring at her in total disbelief. His cronies were laughing at him now and I knew that we were moving into hurricane season.

Realizing I now had no choice but to get into the middle of things, I reluctantly left my drums and shoved my way into the middle of the arena.

"You touch her," I told Jordan, "and I'll hit you so hard your eyeballs are going to squirt out your ears."

Yeah, it had to come down to me and Jordan. He had about fifty pounds more than me on his side and he carried knuckles and maybe a knife. He wouldn't lose any sleep if he killed me. If anything happened to him, he had a very loyal gang with him who would settle up the problem by dismembering me in front of the crowd. So I wasn't exactly the happiest guy on the planet.

I knew Barry was screaming at me to not get involved but his path was blocked by part of the Jordan gang. Craig and Danny were getting up off the floor. Alex was looking for a safe escape route. Kelsey was screaming something at Jordan that was less than complimentary. And I took the first punch hard on my left ear. I felt my brain kind of slide from one side to the other, until I could get my balance. Then I planted a big one in

Jordan's gut, knowing that he was very proud of his bloated pot belly and that this was the place to injure his pride.

Jordan just smiled and reached out with two hands like a pair of lobster claws and tried to get my head into a vice lock. I tripped him, then tried to tromp on his face only he rolled away and pulled me down, then drove a knee into my back. When I found my way back up onto my feet, I hit him in the jaw. He hit me back and I felt the first dribble of blood sliding down my chin. That was when I realized we were both smiling. I hadn't had this kind of fun in a long time.

We were both breathing hard. We heard Eric yelling at us. He had Jeffrey in a headlock. "Guys, you're wasting your energy. Stop hassling each other. Look who I got here. Come on. Have some real fun." I looked at Jordan and suddenly it was like old times. We felt like brothers. We smiled. I'd forgotten all about the music. Eric said, "Come on, Cody, you first. You did it before. You can do it again."

I didn't like that. Now it was out of the can. Kelsey was watching me like a hawk. Okay, okay. I started towards Eric. The least I could do was make him let Jeffrey go. We didn't need this. But I guess Kelsey wasn't so good at reading the look on my face when I had one puffed up eye and a drizzle of blood. Suddenly she charged at me and bit hard on my arm. I yelled and nearly wonked her one but caught myself just in time. She really thought I was going to batter poor Jeffrey.

Well, that's when the cops showed up. They moved towards us through the crowd. Somebody with a megaphone told everyone to leave the building and to get off the property. Our first gig was over.

I tried to just fade on back toward my drums and pretend I wasn't involved. But a pair of cops had circled round and "wanted to talk" to me as well as to Jordan, Eric, Jeffrey, and Kelsey.

One of the policemen recognized Jeffrey. "You want to tell us what was going on here?" he asked.

I wondered then if Jeffrey, too, thought I was ready to trash him . . . to trash him again. He had no reason to believe otherwise, I guess. All he had to do was say the words and I'd be arrested. I realized I was still wearing his stupid watch. He could have nailed Jordan and Eric as well. Typically, Logan had squeezed through some rathole and made it clear of the hall before the cops got us.

I waited for Jeffrey to point the finger and for the police to collar me. "It was all a misunderstanding," he said. "That's all it was."

The same cop looked at Kelsey. "You wanna explain this?"

"It's like he said. It was just a misunderstanding."

I breathed a sigh of relief and rubbed my arm where I felt the indentations left by Kelsey's teeth.

Chapter 11

I didn't see what Alex was so upset about. We actually made money on the gig. The cops cleared everybody out so fast that no one had a chance to ask for their money back. Barry paid off the hall and split the take with us. I felt like a rich man with cash in my jeans. I convinced Kelsey that it was not my intention to bust Jeffrey but to free him.

"Sorry about the damage," she said, pointing to the purple marks left where she had bitten me.

"No problem," I said. "Besides, I kind of like the way it looks."

Barry had to have a meeting with the cops but they never fined him or anything. And thanks to the ruckus, the rep of Scream Static actually increased. What else could you ask for?

Despite all the good news, Alex was still unhappy. "It's costing me too much," he said again. We were trying to practise in Kelsey's garage, trying to get onto a couple more tunes, but Alex was getting cranky.

"Costing you? You made money, didn't you?"

Alex was sore about him and his buds getting pushed around. It made them look like the wimps they really were. "We never should have gotten involved with a loser like Cody. It was all his fault. If it wasn't for him and his friends, the dance would have gone without a hitch," Alex told Kelsey, as if I wasn't right there.

"I thought you liked the element of danger he added to the band," Kelsey said. "Wasn't that the way you put it?"

So there.

"I just didn't know how low we were all going to have to sink, Kelsey. Look, we don't need him. It's your songs that matter. We could get another drummer."

What a douche. Such a pessimist. He couldn't see that we were hot. Everybody knew it. I said nothing, for once. Despite the verbal abuse, I was cool. Kelsey appreciated that.

"Let's take a break," she said. "I'll get you guys some Pepsi's."

"Got any beer?" I asked.

Kelsey couldn't see the humour. She gave me one of her death-ray stares. "My father catches you drinking his beer and you'll find a set of tire treads on your face."

I loved it when she talked to me like that. "What a way with words," I told Alex.

Alex just sulked.

When she was out of range I said, "What's with you? I thought you and I had an agreement?"

"I'd never make any deals with you, Cody."

"Without me, this band would be like stale bread."

"Without me, this band wouldn't exist," Alex said.

Funny thing, but after we argued like that, we actually played better. Get the grudge going, pump up the heat on ticked-off, and suddenly we were cooking.

I started thinking about the fact that some of Kelsey's lyrics were about guys like me — well, guys like Jordan and Eric — and I guess I'd have to include myself. And there I was playing the drums on these tunes that were major put-downs on my attitude.

So much stuff in my head to get me confused. Why didn't Jeffrey turn me in to the cops? Two chances he had and backed down both times. Weak in the knees or something else?

Late at night, I'd lie in my bed and crank on the radio, tune it in to CKDU, the only station in town that played real music. I'd listen to Cuckledoo (our nickname for the station) until they played one of our tunes. We had six tracks down already, all recorded in Barry's basement studio. I was beginning to feel completely at home sitting on his toilet with my clothes on, playing the drums. But listening to our songs on the radio late at night made me dream about making it big.

I decided I'd beat the brains out of Alex if he

kicked me out of the band. He'd have a hard time replacing me. It never occurred to me that he was still thinking of walking out on us. Not with our rep. Kelsey was always trying to convince Alex that I was changing. Of course, I wasn't. It was the same old me. All I had learned was to keep my mouth shut and not rant so much. The only real reason I didn't hang out with the boys anymore was that I just didn't have time. I had music. I had a life.

The garage sessions were getting to be real events. You'd never know who would show up. Barry was there sometimes, just listening. Every once in while he'd throw out a little low-key advice. Sometimes kids from school would come by and hang out in the driveway. Mrs. Dubinski was getting complaints from the neighbours but she didn't like dealing with them, so she just left her phone off the hook when we played.

Alex mellowed once girls started to think he was cool. He had a couple of fans and his grades were slipping. So I figured that maybe he was coming around. But then his old man, who owned an advertising business, got him in touch with some big time music promoter. He had signed some really smooth acts like Humble Heart, Miltonics, and Professor Ouija. Big time stuff but all pretty tame music, stuff like you'd hear on C100.

Alex introduced the spiffy dude with the briefcase as Giles Redmond. The man had a handshake like a vice grip.

"I've heard your music," he said. "I hear potential."

"Cool," I said. "You want to offer us a million bucks?"

Kelsey gave me a death-ray look.

"Not yet," Giles said, cool as frozen mucous. "I'm just saying we're interested. My job is to work the fringes, find bands like yours and groom them for success."

I didn't like that word "groom."

"Meaning?" Kelsey asked.

"Work with you. Fine-tune the music, make suggestions as to how to create a more marketable product."

"What's that supposed to mean?" I snapped.

"Alex and I have been talking," Giles said. "Maybe he can explain."

Alex was all worked up over this guy. They had been hanging out together and I had the feeling Alex had already made some sort of deal.

"It's like this," Alex began. "Giles is willing to work with us, help us write and produce a few tunes as demos and then start playing some gigs, maybe go on tour. This is how it happens. This is the break we've been looking for."

I thought Alex was going to pee his pants. I wondered what Kelsey was thinking but she wasn't showing her cards.

"How much do we get paid?" I asked.

"Nothing at first. We invest some time in you. You invest some time in us. If it works out, we all go home happy."

"No money?"

"Not now. But later . . ." Hands in the air, fluttering dollars of the imagination.

"We already have a manager," Kelsey said. "Barry's been good to us. You heard his work."

"Amateur stuff," Giles said. "If we could get you into a Toronto studio, you'd sound much better."

"When would that be?"

"Depends."

"On what?" she asked.

"On when we get a deal." Giles pulled some CDs out of his briefcase. "These are some of our recording artists," he said. "You can keep these."

It was an impressive looking pile of very successful rockers — Humble Heart, Professor O, Miltonics, Discreet Destroyers, that sort of thing.

"We've got a deal," Alex said.

Kelsey looked worried but said nothing.

I was staring at the CDs and thinking about what it would be like to be as rich as some of those dudes. "Where do I sign?" I asked.

"No contract. Not yet. First we have to see how you respond to our development program."

It sounded like I had just signed up for a bodybuilding course or something. But I didn't care. Hey, I was ready for the next big move. I knew we had it coming.

Chapter 12

Around school, kids talked about the band and about our only live performance that had lasted for all of four songs. And it was like everybody was waiting for us to do something big.

I woke up one Saturday morning feeling lonely and hungry. I immediately went over to Kelsey's thinking I could bum a decent breakfast. Kelsey's father was off playing golf and her mom was sleeping in, so she seemed to enjoy my company. I asked her if she'd mind making me some eggs and maybe a dozen pieces of bacon.

"Sure," she said. "No problem." She took a whole pack of raw bacon out of the fridge, slipped it out of the wrapper and said, "Hold out your hands."

I was thinking she was going to hand me a plate but instead she handed me this big greasy wad of bacon.

"You like it raw, don't you?" she said. "You said you wanted eggs too?"

"No thanks," I said, putting the bacon back in its wrapper and wiping my hands off on the tablecloth. "I'll just make myself some toast."

That's when Kelsey opened up the *Chronicle Herald* and discovered our good fortune. A story on page eight said that a bunch of parents had declared our music to be "insulting, obscene, and dangerous." Three sweeter words had never found their way into the English language. These goodhearted, upstanding adults called themselves Parents for Musical Morality.

According to some lady named Mary Montgomery, "The Condom Song" showed a "serious lack of respect for authority and promoted promiscuity in teenagers." Mrs. Montgomery had heard her fourteen-year-old daughter listening to the song on the Internet. And Mrs. Morality Montgomery proceeded to go through the roof. She found an ally in the form of Richard Garber, another parent whose son had been warped out of his morality by our music and was forever damaged because he had listened to the lyrics of "Downtown Dangerous."

"It's censorship again," Kelsey said. "They can't do this."

"Of course they can," I said, spraying fragments of toast around the room as I talked. "If people like to hate our music, it means we must be doing something right."

"How come the paper didn't ask us to comment?"

"Kelsey, don't get so serious about this. It's just

a bunch of old geeks with hormonal deficiency trying to stop us from having fun."

"Yeah, but they're also trying to censor us."

"Let 'em. Kids love anything their parents say is bad for them."

"Yeah, but the Parents for Musical Morality are going to be on our case whatever we do. And they're going to try to have CKDU's broadcasting licence revoked."

"I'll bust their legs," I said.

"You always revert to being a caveman when you're upset, don't you?" Kelsey never knew when I was joking. But then neither did I.

"What's wrong with that?"

"Nothing a good brain transplant wouldn't cure," she said. The way she said it really ticked me off. I was getting tired of Kelsey putting me down all the time. She still couldn't accept me for who I was, and that really bugged me. When would she give it up and stop trying to turn me into something I wasn't?

While I was sulking, Barry called to say he'd read the story and was still behind us a hundred percent. We hadn't said much to Barry since Giles had shown up, but now that he had called us, I guess Kelsey felt it was time to give him the lowdown. "Come on over to our jam session this afternoon," Kelsey told him. "There's somebody I think you should meet."

That somebody was Giles. I knew this was going to be awkward. But Kelsey figured that together,

Barry and Giles could help us plan a counterattack on the PFMM.

While we were setting up, Alex said his mom had friends who were joining this musical morality thing.

"Alex, it doesn't mean you have to worry about it. She's only your mother," I said.

"You don't know how much flak I put up with to stay in this band."

"My heart is bleeding big puddles of blood for you, Alex. But grow out of it. What your mom's friends think doesn't mean squat. They're all gonna be dead in forty years and we're all going to still be hammering music."

Barry arrived a short while later. He was running in full support mode. "Yeah, man. Don't let it get to you. They start censoring your songs and who knows where it will end. You can't stop writers and musicians from being creative by putting limits on what they are allowed to say. It's freedom of speech."

I was afraid this was going to get real boring. I was afraid he'd get all wired up in one of his political tirades and we'd have to listen to it. So I made a musical comment by doing a heavy roll on the snare drum. Barry took the hint, looking a little hurt.

"Just trying to loosen up my wrists, man. Sorry."

"You don't need to apologize," Barry said.

"I'm going to write a song directed right at these self-righteous music-haters," Kelsey asserted.

"I don't know," Alex said. "I just don't know. It doesn't feel right."

I didn't get what he was talking about. Of course it felt right. A song that trashed a bunch of lame prudes was an excellent idea. I knew Kelsey would make it good and angry, which would give me a chance to come up with a really pounding beat.

And then there was Giles. Giles didn't take off his shades when he came inside the garage. Giles wore shoes that probably cost more than my whole drum set. He had a snotty way of hanging out that told me he thought he was really very important.

Barry sized him up like a mortal enemy. He introduced himself.

"I've heard about your work with the band," Giles told Barry. "You've done good. D and D respects guys like you who help out with the first step in a career."

"Right."

"The band has told you about my interest?"

"Well, I knew something was up," Barry said. "We've been working together. I've been acting as a manager but we don't have any formal arrangements. I believe in these guys. Whatever they want for their career is okay by me."

That was typical Barry. Never pushy. Giles was honing in on territory Barry had carved out for himself. Old Barry had invested his time and moola in us and we were ready to leave him in the dust for D and D. But the dude didn't seem to mind. Maybe he was just a born wimp.

"Have you seen this?" Barry asked. He handed Giles a copy of the *Herald*.

Giles dipped his glasses. He read the words slowly, moving his lips, just like me when I read.

Alex tried to get his guitar in tune to Kelsey's keyboard but he was having a hard time of it. I knew something was bothering him. I was getting really tired of sitting there doing nothing. "Let's do some music," I said.

"I'm not in tune," Alex snapped.

"So what?"

"Can you give us a minute, Cody?" Kelsey interjected.

I took a break and walked outside. I was tired of being polite. Our fame now rested on the fact that we were considered insulting, obscene, and dangerous. We should start living up to that image. Who would care if we were in tune?

Barry borrowed Alex's guitar to help him get it locked in tune. That's when Giles sidled over to me outside on the driveway.

"This thing in the paper is not so good for you," he said, all confidential now, like he was telling me some hot new secret.

I almost laughed. "It isn't?" I asked.

"The company will not look favourably on bad publicity. Not at this stage of your career, anyway."

"Why not?"

"Because you're going to alienate that whole audience who would listen to you on commercial stations."

"But I thought a bad rep was good."

He shook his head. "A bad rep is good if you've

already established a good rep as being bad, in the musical sense, before you cross over to being bad in the real world, where maybe you break a law or something."

It sounded like double-talk to me. "No kidding?"

"No kidding. Look, Cody, I can tell you're a reasonable guy with a level head."

He had me pegged right down to the wire.

"That's why I'm going to ask you to help me with this one. Persuade Kelsey that Scream Static needs some material that is more commercial, something that won't offend anyone. Just plain music. You have good musical abilities. You three carve a weird and intriguing image. All you need is the right material. Don't let the language turn off a huge chunk of your potential audience."

"You're messing with my head," I told him.

"Listen. Let's be straight. What do you want out of your career? You wanna play music just for your friends or do you want to be in front of big crowds, maybe record in the best studios in North America and make big bucks?"

"I'd say the big bucks thing sounds like a good choice."

"Good," said Giles. "Now we're speaking the same language. Alex is already with me on this one. But I thought you could help me with Kelsey. You know how she is."

"Sure," I said. "I'll try to sweet talk her on this one."

I didn't really know what I was agreeing to. I

mean, the guy had a good point — about the money and stuff. I still didn't care about the words in the songs. I had my eye on the end of the rainbow and I didn't want to get off course.

Alex and Kelsey were finally in tune. Barry was sitting on some boxes in the corner.

"I'm gonna be sending a sample of your work soon to T.O.," Giles said to Kelsey. "I think we have a fair sampling of your rough stuff but I'd like you to come up with a couple of tunes that aren't quite so far off the centre."

"What's that supposed to mean?" Kelsey asked.

"You know. Something more commercial, more pop. They'll want to hear a balance of songs. They'll want to know if you're a one-hit wonder or a versatile band that can be groomed."

There was that dog word again. Yuck.

"I had a couple of ideas I've been working on," Alex jumped in. "Listen to these chord riffs."

Alex whipped off some basic chord structures and suggested a rhythm to me. It was kind of light, kind of air-head danceable but I found myself going along for the ride. Giles was smiling now. Alex was smiling. Barry and Kelsey were looking at us like we had just transformed into the Lunenburg Polka Band. I knew exactly what had happened just then. Alex and Giles had come up with a little plan. I had joined the conspiracy and we were heading one step closer to the middle of the road.

Giles had his glasses off. He winked at me now. I felt like I had just let the Prunepits for Morality have a cause to celebrate. But, hey, it was just a temporary compromise. And I was willing to go for it if it meant getting a contract with D and D. It wasn't like selling out or anything. It was just learning the ropes.

Kelsey hammered on a whole pile of keys at once. "What is this putrid slop?" she screeched.

"It was sounding good," Giles said.

"Come on, Kelsey," Alex complained. "You always initiate all the songs. I'd like some input for once. Let's roll with this. You and I can write the lyrics. We can work on it."

"I don't like it," she said. "It's not us."

"We have to learn to grow — creatively, I mean," Alex said.

"This isn't growing. This is something else."

"I say we do a few more commercial tunes that Giles can send to T.O. with the other stuff," Alex said.

"And I say we don't back down for anybody. We stick to our style of music."

"Okay," Alex said. "Let's take a vote."

It was democracy in action. Only problem was there were three of us. Alex was on one side of the barbed wire fence. Kelsey was on the other. And my butt was squarely on the ragged metal edge of the top wire.

"I'm with Alex," I said. Sure, I felt like a traitor — big time. But I figured it would be worth it in the long run.

So Giles paid Barry to record us again in his

basement — two new tunes that Alex wrote, with some coaching from Giles. Kelsey wrote the lyrics but Giles took an axe to them and changed them around so they sounded like a lot of that drippy nonsense on C100. Kelsey wasn't pleased but she went along with it grudgingly. Giles made the promise that if we could get our foot in the door, then we could go back to doing anything we wanted to. The only difference was that we'd be getting some real gigs, we'd be making some real money, and we'd be on the road to rock music heaven.

The tunes were bland, the music so-so, and the drumming like something out of a can. But Giles loved it and sent the noise off to Toronto.

Meanwhile, Giles had met with the PFMM and told them about our new direction. He told us it was "damage control" but he wouldn't tell us exactly what he had said to them. The Morality Squad quieted down a bit but suddenly CKDU was playing a lot less of our two big hits.

Chapter 13

Giles wanted to celebrate. He made it sound like we were headed for the big time. I thought we'd have like a real wild party or something. Instead, he took us out to a restaurant called The New World. They didn't have anything but foreign food. Nothing real — no pizza, no burgers, no fried chicken. Kelsey thought it was cool but I thought it sucked. It was very boring, let me tell you. I bowed out at about nine o'clock, thinking I could at least get out into the night, maybe run into some action. Anything to get away from wonky food and tea that smelled like perfume.

I knew that if we made it big, we'd get to play major gigs. Then we'd trash hotel rooms and stuff like that. If Kelsey and Alex weren't into it, then I'd have to rely on my fan club to help me out. This was the sort of thing going on in my head as I headed downtown. Despite the boring meal, I was thinking about my glorious career — what I'd wear on stage, how the girls would react, whether or not to get a tattoo of a snake on my forehead. That sort of thing.

Nothing was happening in front of the library. I guess Jordan and the boys had found a new haunt. A couple of cops, looking bored, sat in a squad car shovelling donuts into themselves.

I thought I'd just walk on down through the old cemetery before I headed home. It was dark and spooky, surrounded by tall trees. After sitting in a boring restaurant, I needed something with a taste of weirdness and danger. I opened the gate and walked the path leading past a huge dark statue, past the lines of tombstones. I couldn't hear anything at first except gravel crunching under my feet, but then there was a noise — a scream.

I stopped. There was the sound of someone getting hit — hit hard. I heard him groan from the pain. I heard somebody else laugh. The laugh told the whole story. I'd recognize the sound of Logan getting his fun anywhere.

Slowly I walked closer, staying behind some bushes so I wouldn't be seen. Why didn't I just go right up to them and join in? I'd played this scene before. What was holding me back?

Now, though, it was all different. I wasn't a part of it. I was what you'd call an innocent (or not-so-innocent) bystander. I didn't know who was being trashed. Could have been some homeless fag. They were known to hang out in this place sometimes.

They were also known to get beat up here. Jordan, Eric, and Logan had always talked about how much fun it would be to do an honest-to-god stakeout. I reckon tonight was their night.

Keeping my distance, I stayed behind some bushes and shifted around so I could get a good view of what was happening. There was only a little street light getting through the branches but I got the picture clear enough. A guy was down, curled up like a baby now. The only sound he made was from the air coming out of his mouth in short bursts when Eric kicked him in the gut. I heard Jordan talking to the guy, telling him he deserved what he got, telling him that this was some sort of lesson.

What happened in my head just then is pretty hard to explain. Maybe I'd been hanging out with Kelsey too much, listening to the lyrics of her songs. I wanted to turn around and get out of there. I didn't want any part of this scene. The words of "Downtown Dangerous" were jammed inside my head, haunting me more than any cemetery ghost could.

I felt confused and a little crazy. Then I edged further left and got a good look at the maniacal smile on Logan's face. I watched as he kicked the guy in the chest as hard as he could, backed off, turned around, and did it again. He did it as if in some kind of a dance. He did it to entertain Eric and Jordan. This wasn't like the beating we gave Jeffrey in front of the public library. There was no one else around here. I had no idea how long this had been going on. And it was just like Logan to keep a thing like this going until . . . until when?

Jordan and Eric had probably already grounded the guy, knocked the wind out of him, and started to bash his head in. Logan's idea of fun was to finish somebody off. Before, we'd always been interrupted. We'd always had to split before we got caught.

That wasn't going to happen here, I suddenly realized. I saw Jordan reach down and punch the guy in the head. They weren't going to quit. Maybe they were going to kill him.

I felt sick to my stomach. I wanted to run away from there real bad. I didn't want to be around to see it. I didn't want to get involved. The ugly thing was that I knew I'd been part of this scene. But what about now? Run, said the voice inside me. Just get the hell out of here and don't tell anyone what you saw. It's not your responsibility.

But my feet didn't want to run. Instead, I made some noise. I scuffed my shoes in the gravel. I cleared my throat. I rustled the bushes. No way was I going to show myself but I was counting on the fact that my old buddies hadn't changed. They loved to get their fun, but they sure as heck didn't want to get collared for it.

Would they come after me or would they just hightail it?

"Who's there?" Logan asked.

I didn't say anything. That would be best. I

was breathing hard. Let them think someone was watching but don't let them know if it's one person or two. Above all, don't let them know it's me.

Eric walked in my direction but he couldn't see me. What little light there was came from behind me. I could see him, though. And I could see that he was scared now. Scared that he'd get caught in the act.

He didn't say anything. He turned. "Let's get out of here," he told Jordan.

The three of them ran off towards the cemetery gate. They were running hard and they were running fast. Sometimes we'd just take our time and kind of jog away from the scene of the crime. But this was different. I knew what that meant. If they were this scared, it was because they had done some real damage. The price would be high if they were caught. That's why they were running fast, running scared from anyone who might confront them, anyone who could pin the blame.

They were gone. I was still standing behind the bushes, maybe five metres from where this guy was curled up on the ground. Now what? Hadn't I done my bit? Why wasn't I getting out of there too?

It was crazy but I had to see how bad off this guy was. I slowly walked towards him. "You all right?" was all I could say.

There was no answer. I hunched down and got a look. Blood on the face. Arms still gripped around his gut. "You okay, man?" I asked. Stupid question. Again no answer. He was unconscious.

I leaned over. I think he was breathing but it was too hard to tell because I was panting and my heart was pounding away. A new fear gripped me. If anyone found me here now, I'd get blamed for this. It would be easy to pin the blame on me. Run, that voice inside me said.

But I also knew that if I left him here like this, he might not be found. I was sure that if he didn't get help right away, this guy was going to die. I couldn't let that happen.

"I'll get help," I told him, even though I knew he couldn't hear. I reached in my pocket for my cell phone but it wasn't there. I'd run out of cell phone minutes and hadn't bothered to bring it.

Man, I never felt more scared or more responsible for someone else's life! I tripped twice as I tried to make it back to the street. I thought of running up to the cops on Spring Garden Road, hoping they'd still be parked there. But it was too far away, maybe too much of a risk for me. The near-lifeless image of that guy back there kept jumping up inside my head.

I found a phone and dialed 911.

I told the man who answered about the scene in the cemetery. I told him exactly where to go.

"He needs help bad. Send an ambulance. Do it quick, man. I'm serious."

The voice on the other end was calm. "I got it. Stay on the line." I heard him fire off the location over the radio to a cruiser. Then he was back on the line. "Okay," he said to me. "We've got somebody on the way. You want to tell me your name?"

I held onto the phone for a second and looked at it. Then I slammed down the receiver. No way were they going to get my name.

But it still wasn't over for me. I was afraid they might not find him. It was a dark night and it was a big cemetery. So I ran back to the beat-up guy. He was still on the ground, not moving. "It's okay," I found myself telling him. "I got help."

I stayed there with him. I didn't do anything but I stayed there until I heard footsteps hurrying towards us. Then I sneaked back into the bushes and ducked down low. First, there were two cops. They checked him over. One guy started giving mouth-to-mouth through a tube. Then two other men arrived with a stretcher. When the guy was carried away, the cops stayed behind and shone their flashlights in all directions. I had to stay low and quiet but when they moved away a little to pick up something on the ground, I turned and ran like crazy.

They heard me. "Stop!" one of them yelled, but I never turned around. I ran again into the night. I wasn't going to be around to talk to any cops. I ran just like I had done before. Only now something was different. I was still scared, I was still running, but it felt more like I was running away from myself than running away from the cops.

Chapter 14

I kept a low profile over the weekend. I didn't show up for practice on Saturday. I sat in my room and listened to music and watched movies on the Internet. My mother kept asking me to do stuff around the house, but I told her to get lost.

"If you don't want to do what your mother tells you," my dad confided, "don't say you won't do it. Just say you're busy and you'll get around to it later. Maybe she'll forget she asked you and everybody will be happy. I know I shouldn't tell you this, but it's how your mother and I get along. You've got to learn how to handle women, son."

Great advice from my old man. I said I'd try to stick by it.

The business about the guy getting beat up was a pretty big deal. It was all over the news. He nearly died. The news anchor on TV referred to me as "the unidentified caller, a young male who saved the man's life."

Maybe I should have felt like a hero. But I didn't. Not by a long shot. I was full of really mixed up feelings, full of a kind of anger — anger at my old gang, mainly, but also anger at me. Why exactly was I mad at myself over this?

When I put my fist through the wallboard in my room, my mother was pretty upset. She said I did it because those movies I was watching were such a bad influence.

"Tell your mother you're sorry and that you'll fix it," my father said.

"I'm sorry," I said. "I'll fix it later, okay?"

I went out for a walk and found myself stopping in front of a newspaper box. The headline in the *Chronicle Herald* read, "Thugs Strike in City Cemetery." I bought a paper and sat down to read the story. The victim had recovered enough to give an interview to the papers. He said he'd been sleeping in the cemetery when he was attacked by "young punks." The police talked about "teenage violence" and "street gangs." They had statistics about the increase in fights and about people being attacked, but it all seemed to be missing something. There was one question screaming at me: Why were we doing these things? I knew all about how it had happened. I knew how I felt. I knew what Jordan, Eric, and Logan must have been thinking the other night. But I didn't know why we felt that way. Up until now I had never cared.

We liked being angry, and it felt good to trash something or someone. Now I was beginning to see what a loser I'd been.

The TV and newspaper reporters didn't understand anything about this. I kicked hard at the glass in the newspaper box. It was plastic. It didn't break, which made me even angrier, so I kicked it over and stomped on it hard until the side was nicely dented in. Feeling only slightly better, I went back home, back to my room. No more newspapers, no more TV. All I had in my room in the way of drums was one old snare drum. I started playing and didn't quit until it was dark and my parents had left the house to get some peace and quiet.

On Sunday, in Kelsey's garage, she gave me hell for missing practice on Saturday, but she said it wasn't all a waste. She'd conned Alex into working on a new tune — something like their old stuff. Alex had gone along with it to make her happy.

Giles wasn't around. He'd flown to Toronto to push a demo to the bigwigs at D and D. So Kelsey had reverted to her old ways. She'd written a really hard, pounding tune with some angry lyrics and lots of swearing. It took me no time at all to come up with the right percussion to fit. I couldn't really hear the words but I knew I liked the song.

On the fifth try, we got it tight. When the wailing guitar lead and the crashing cymbal began to fade at the end, I discovered we had an audience. Barry.

"Giles is going to hate it," he said. He was smiling.

"It's only one song," Kelsey said. "If he doesn't like it, it's his problem. We can do other stuff, too. He doesn't have to approve of everything we do."

"But I thought you'd already gone commercial. I thought you left this original stuff behind."

"No way," Kelsey said.

"Well," Alex corrected. "We have to try new material. Kelsey came up with this. It was important to her, so we worked on it. Gotta keep everyone happy, right?"

"Right," Barry said. "Can we record it tonight? While it's still fresh?"

"Yes," Kelsey said instantly. I sensed conspiracy here.

"Maybe we shouldn't," Alex objected.

"I say we do it," I said immediately. It was two out of three again. I felt bad about having pushed Barry off to the sidelines and letting Giles have so much say. We couldn't do wimp-out music all the time.

It wasn't until I got out from behind the drums in Barry's bathroom and got a listen to the first mix that I realized what the song was about. It was about the incident in the cemetery. Kelsey had told the story almost like she'd been there, like she'd seen it happen. She was good and mad about what had happened and angrier than I'd ever heard her.

Kelsey was smiling and looking straight at me as we finished the recording.

"Now that is a song," Barry said.

"It's too controversial," Alex insisted. "I don't

want it to go beyond this. It's going to turn people against us again. Look at the language. Those Morality Moms are gonna be unhappy. And what about the creeps who do the stuff you're talking about, Kelsey? They're going to be offended and come looking for us." Alex sounded like a real noodle now. "Besides, Giles would hate this."

"We've already established that Giles would hate it," Kelsey snapped. "So what?"

"So we have our careers to think about."

I wasn't getting involved in the conflict but I knew what it was coming down to. One said yes, one said no.

"Alex is right," I said. "It could be bad for our careers." But I wasn't really thinking about careers. I was thinking about the violence issue. I didn't want to get involved in it. It was all too close to home.

Kelsey walked over to me now. She grabbed the drumsticks out of my hand and glared.

"What is this, a threat?" I asked.

She took the sticks and tapped out something like a code on the watch on my wrist.

"Take it any way you want," she said.

"It's okay," Barry said, sounding really disappointed. "We can just save it in the can. When you hit the big time, I can just listen to it for my own private enjoyment and realize what might have been."

I was looking for a way out of this. I pretended it wasn't Kelsey but Barry who had just changed my mind. "Ah, what the heck. We put all this time into it. Let's send a few copies around town. Maybe see if Cuckledoo radio wants to play it. What can it hurt?"

"No, dammit," Alex said. "Absolutely not. Kelsey, you lied to me. You said if we worked this one up, if I went along, just for you, you'd have it out of your system so we could work on some more commercial tunes. There's no way I'm going to let any of you release this."

But nothing Alex said stopped us. It went to Jeffrey at CKDU and he persuaded the guys there to play "Back off, Bashers!" every hour for forty-eight hours straight. It grabbed hold of the attention of enough kids in town to make it the talk of the street and the talk of the school.

What's weird is that you'd think that because it was a song putting down violence, a lot of adults would have liked it. But that wasn't the case. Some very strict religious parents caught their kids listening to the song and blew the whistle on us, calling us "obscene (again), insulting (again), and (of course) dangerous to the minds of youth." The Parents For Musical Morality resurfaced, and actually picketed CKDU.

There were editorials against us now in the papers and, in some bizarre way, people were linking the anger in Kelsey's song — the anger against violence — with the violence itself. PFMM wanted the press to believe our music was somehow responsible. We were, as they claimed, dangerous.

Our music should be banned — in schools, on the radio, and on the Internet.

Alex was angry alright, but not about the same things as Kelsey. If anybody asked me, I didn't say anything about the tune but, "Hey man, it's only a song. It doesn't mean nothin'." I liked playing it stupid. It was an easy way out and it allowed me to roll with all the punches. None of the people who were complaining got to me, though.

Well, that's not quite true. One of the critics did. Jordan. Jordan called me up late one night to say, "Cody, I know exactly what you've become now. You're a bloody traitor. We want you to know that we hate your song, man. We think you've been brainwashed. We feel sorry for you, brud. We think you should be careful, you know. Real careful."

There was nothing to say so I just hung up. Because of our song, I was now publicly connected with what had happened in the cemetery that night. Once again I thought about how I'd crossed the line. The Cody I once was no longer existed. I was this other person. Here I was, late at night standing in the darkness of my house, wondering who I was, what was going to happen next in this crazy mess, and just how dangerous this whole game had become.

Chapter 15

"You blew it," Giles said when he walked into the garage.

"Giles, we came up with a piece of music that means something to people," said Kelsey in defence of our action. "We said what no one else in this city was willing to say."

There was this spooked look on Alex's face. I knew just what he was thinking. I was thinking it too — career down the tubes. All because we tried to humour Kelsey. Or was it more than that?

"Giles, it was a mistake," Alex said. "Nothing more."

"Well, I can't afford those kind of mistakes. You know, I'm really disappointed you guys didn't consult with me first on this one. There I was up in T.O. making the pitch for Scream Static to open for a couple of big acts. I played those new tracks you did. You guys started out rough but were moving in the right direction. But now this."

Giles held his sunglasses in his hand and looked out the driveway. There were some kids cruising by on skateboards — little punk kids like I used to beat on. When they saw us set up in the garage, one kid in a loud yellow shirt yelled out, "'Back Off, Bashers!' — good tune. Way to go, dudes." His buddies howled in a kind of hound-dog sound that meant they liked the song as well.

I smiled, but Giles didn't see the point. He picked up a rock and chucked it in their direction. It skidded down the driveway and caught the wheels of one of the skateboards, then bounced into the side of his own car parked at the curb. I nearly broke out laughing.

Giles tried to get control of himself. He rubbed his forehead and said, "I'm thinking of cutting my losses and running."

"You can't do that," said Alex. "We made one little mistake."

"One big mistake," Giles corrected. "I don't want this kind of badass publicity. Especially not from a green band — one that doesn't even have a contract."

Screw the contract, I was ready to say. I didn't know if I could put up with any more of this creep's lecture. Fame, fortune, and wrecking hotel rooms suddenly seemed like a fading dream.

"But I've already invested a lot of time in you guys. You know what my time is worth on an hourly basis?"

No one ventured at a figure. My guess was that his time was worth squat, but he obviously thought he was one hot music promoter.

"Maybe we can do damage control again," he continued, pacing about the garage. "I can donate some money to that campus radio station and request they pull the tune. If we can nip this thing right here in Halifax, it won't go any further. No more airplay and maybe we can calm down the morality people. And I know you already put some of this stuff on the Internet, so you're gonna have to get it off there as well."

"So it's back to censorship," Kelsey said, her arms crossed in front of her.

Giles pointed a finger at her now. "Look, do you want to throw it all away? You want to stay a garage band forever? How much money are you making now? How many gigs have you lined up? You think Barry is going to do you guys any good?" Giles was all revved up now. "Barry doesn't know anything about the music business. I do. I know how things work. I know two things: I know what it takes to make it in this business and I know you guys have what it takes. But I'm going to need you to commit yourself to my game plan, go along with my decisions."

He put his shades back on. That was good because it looked as if his eyeballs were about to pop out of his skull like a cartoon character's.

"Giles is right," Alex said. "Look, he's giving us another shot. Let's take it."

"Censorship and all?" Kelsey asked Alex, but she was staring at Giles.

"It's compromise, that's all," Alex said. "It's business."

I was thinking, Oh no. Here we go again. Democracy in action. Man, my head was messed up. I was still thinking about the poor guy who got beat up. I was thinking about me getting involved. I had already taken a stand for something. What, I don't know. But now there was this other stuff. If I said the wrong thing here, I was maybe going to lose the music, lose another band and my only shot at making it big.

Kelsey was looking at me and she looked uncertain, worried. "I don't know if I can do it," she said.

What did she want out of me? Why was she looking at me? "Sure," I said, trying to reassure her. "You can do it. We all can."

That was the way it was. She wanted me to say it was okay to go along with Giles. I mean, the guy was really putting the screws to us. If he walked now, then, like he said, it would be a big waste. No more chance at the big time.

"I've gotta have an answer. I've gotta hear it from all of you. I need a hundred percent or I'm out of here. No more games."

Games. The word stuck in my head. That's what my life had been up to now. Games. Always games. Bullying people, beating up on them. Hanging out with Jordan and the boys. Was it time to get serious? Time to grow up? Or was it one more stupid game?

I looked at Giles. He was staring at me from behind his hundred-dollar sunglasses. The lyrics to Kelsey's song went through my head and seeing my image in the mirrors of Giles shades — what I saw at first was me sitting at my drums.

Then I saw me crouching over the beat-up slob in the cemetery.

I was supposed to say something now, supposed to say I was in, that I was serious, willing to go along for the ride.

Instead I said, "I can't do it, Giles. And neither can Kelsey."

Kelsey looked stunned. "What are you doing? You can't answer for me."

"Sorry, babe."

But Kelsey didn't have to say anything more.

"I don't freaking believe this!" Giles screamed.

"Believe it," I said.

"Cody, you're out of your mind!" Alex shouted at me.

"I'm sorry, Giles. I really am. But I've never been very good at going along with the crowd. Besides, I'm too lazy to make a career out of anything. I just like to play drums, man. I didn't want to get serious. I didn't know about all this business bullshit."

Alex looked like he was having a hard time breathing. I knew what it was all about, but I didn't have to come out and say it. I knew where Kelsey had been coming from all along. And now I wasn't about to let her back down. What I was really saying didn't have to be said.

"Cody is right," Kelsey said now, smiling at me — for the first time looking like she really had a thing for me. "I think I'm lazy too. Career sounds too much like work. I think we'll just keep doing what we're doing."

That was the end for Giles. That was the end for Alex too. With them went our shot at a million dollars and a chance to trash hotel rooms across North America.

I can't say I blame Alex. He knew what he wanted and he didn't give up. Within a week he got together with a couple of older guys from a band called Prime Target that had just broken up. They redid those two commercial tunes Alex and Kelsey had worked on. Giles got interested, trying to pick up some of the time he had "invested" in Scream Static. Maybe Alex would still get what he wanted.

That left Kelsey and me. Since my little speech, we had become good "friends." I wanted more than that. She knew it. All she could say was, "Cody, I didn't think I'd ever hear myself say it, but I respect you now."

Respect was not what I was interested in.

We spent a lot of time together. Still doing music, still practising. In the mind of our faithful local audience, Scream Static still existed. Our songs were still getting airplay on the university stations.

And we were getting tons of hits on MySpace. But a band without a guitar is like a horse without legs. Very lame.

Kelsey and I worked up a tune called "Sell-Out," about Giles and D and D and how we saw the commercial music industry. Boy, we were good at alienating people. We figured that if we had already cut some ice by being a controversial band then we needed to keep up our image.

Barry lined up a buddy of his, Warren, to sit in on guitar and work on the tune. I could tell from what I heard, sitting in the bathroom with my drums, that it was pretty weak. The lyrics were good, the song was decent, and Barry thought the tracks were slick. But it was too tame. Without Alex's wild, wailing guitar leads, we just weren't a band. Warren was used to playing jazz, not real music, so I didn't hold it against him.

The new tune also snagged some CKDU airplay. Those guys still thought we were hot, even though we weren't.

About this time, everything began to fade. People were starting to lose interest in the street violence problem. I think all the hoods in the city were keeping cool for a while with all the legal eyes out to nail them.

We tried a few guitar players but they weren't what we needed. Our old rep attracted some guys with no talent and large egos and we always said thanks but no thanks. Despite the fact that our music was still out there, the band had ceased to exist.

As our music faded, so did my so-called relationship with Kelsey. I took her out to the movies once but she wouldn't let me do anything more than put my arm around her.

"Cody, I still think we're just too far apart in our thinking."

"How can you say that, babe?" I asked her outside the theatre beneath the glow of a solitary street light.

"Takes a long time to change an attitude."

Things went a little arctic after that. I walked her home, she pecked me on the cheek with a kiss that said zero, and then I went walking again.

I felt hurt, what can I say?

No babe, no band, no boys. I was alone and it felt rotten. I was nobody — an empty, unhappy guy walking around the city at night. I panhandled to get enough to buy a small bottle of vodka and that went down pretty smooth, but all too soon it was gone.

Jordan, Eric, and Logan were nowhere to be found. I tried the library. I tried the cemetery. I tried some other hangouts. The boys must have been lying low. Maybe I was ready to beg forgiveness and hope they'd ask me back in the family. Maybe I was tired of being off the street and I missed the action. If Jordan wanted to try and smash my face, just let him. It'd been a while but I was ready for a fight. In fact, I think I needed one just to clear my head.

I sat down and nursed a coffee and a double

glazed at Tim Horton's. A couple of punks recognized me as the drummer from SS and said something about how sick our music sounded.

I told them to leave me alone or else I'd waste them. And that was the end of that.

Chapter 16

I knew that the whole music thing was down the tubes. Scream Static was dead.

I was back to bashing a snare drum in my bedroom or sitting around with my headphones or just stewing over what might have been. I tried phoning Kelsey plenty of times but she wasn't there and either her mother wasn't in the mood to take a message or her father just told me I shouldn't phone so much because he was waiting for some business calls.

I felt really out of it at school so I cut a couple of days. The first day I walked around Halifax but the place didn't feel like home anymore. I had an attitude and I was looking for trouble. When I passed the convenience store owned by the Lebanese family, I thought again about busting in the window or doing something serious. I thought it might cure me, but then I figured, what's the point? Why waste the energy? I just kept on walking.

The second day, I just stayed home and holed up in my room, watching music videos on the Internet. I was beginning to wish I'd never joined up with Kelsey and Alex. It was their fault I felt like this. They had let me down. Even Kelsey — the one person in the world I really cared about, the only girl who ever really got through to me.

Late that afternoon the doorbell rang. My mom was out shopping. I went downstairs figuring that whoever it was, I'd give him a hard time. Paper boy, maybe, or a salesman. I'd make him wish he hadn't picked my house.

It was Kelsey.

"Hi," she said.

"Wassup?"

"Thought we should talk."

"Right."

She shrugged. "Well, it's more than that. Thought we should go somewhere together."

"Why?"

"I want to show you something."

"Like?"

"Like you have to come with me. You'll see."

"Where are we going?"

"I want you to meet some people."

"Like a party?"

"Not exactly."

"Exactly what, then?"

She didn't answer. So I gave up. We were starting to sound like those contestants on the stupid game shows.

We walked. She led — I followed — all the way to Argyle Street. We came to a crowd of kids hanging out in front of the drugstore.

"Guys, this is Cody," she said introducing me to a pretty low-life looking bunch of kids. I didn't know their names but I'd seen them around. They lived on and off the street, but mostly on. This was a mixed crowd — every colour, every persuasion. It made me feel kind of itchy to get out of there.

Then I saw the guy I least wanted to see.

"I think you know Jeffrey," Kelsey said.

"Yo," I said.

"How ya doing, Cody?"

The guy reached out to shake my hand. No way. I pulled my hand back. I grabbed onto my wrist. The damn watch. I was still wearing Jeffrey's watch. I pulled my sleeve down over it. What was this supposed to be, some kind of guilt trip?

I felt the walls go up. I didn't want to deal with these people. What was Kelsey trying to prove? "What are we doing here?" I demanded. "You don't want to hang out with these losers."

The other kids were staring at me now. And I was glaring back at them. Yeah, they knew who I was and who I hung out with. I wasn't sure, but maybe I'd trashed more than just Jeffrey in the past. I never thought much of the street kids. Jordan and me had our fun jerking them around on occasion.

Kelsey didn't answer. Instead, one of her girl-friends did — some girl with heavy black eye makeup and droopy hair. She obviously thought she'd be tough, be cool, by giving me a hard time. "Yeah, Kelsey, why did you bring him down here?"

The other kids laughed. Man, I hate being laughed at. If these guys weren't careful, I was going to smash some faces.

Jeffrey saw me clenching my fists. He knew what I was all about. He'd had the unfortunate luck to catch me at a bad moment before. "It's okay, Cody," he said. "You don't need to be afraid of us."

That just about did it. The volcano was ready to cut loose. He was trying to prove he wasn't afraid of me. I was thinking I'd correct that notion.

Kelsey was tugging me away, though. "Relax, Cody. I just wanted you to meet some of my friends. I didn't say they were going to move in with you."

When we were away from there, I wanted an explanation. "Why would you want to hang out with a bunch of losers like that? Those people are worthless. They've got nothing. They're worth nothing. They're not like us."

Kelsey stopped dead in her tracks and grabbed onto my arm. "That was your last chance, Cody. I was really hoping you'd changed. Just a little. I thought there was hope. I really wanted to believe you were human underneath all that tough-guy stuff. But I was wrong. You're still stubborn and pigheaded. Even the music didn't teach you anything. Goodbye."

Maybe I should have just let her walk. It was

hard to believe I let her push me that far and not react. Then, as I watched her walk away, I started thinking that she had been the only really good thing in my life. She had led me to something in music that I had never had before. I had this feeling that if she walked, everything walked. For good.

"Wait." I ran after her. "What is it you want out of me, anyway?" I pleaded.

There was a moment of uncomfortable silence while she stared right at me. Then she opened up. I listened while she told me all the things about myself that had been turning over in my brain for the past weeks — ever since the cemetery, ever since the gig, maybe ever since the night we beat up Jeffrey. It was like she could read me — my past, my present, who knows, maybe my future.

I would have done anything for Kelsey at that moment. And I did. I went back and apologized to all of those kids on Argyle Street. "Sorry," I said to Jeffrey and the others who were still standing there. "Real sorry." But I didn't look straight at anyone.

"Now that you've left such a good impression on them, I think we can go," Kelsey said. "We've got another stop."

She was holding my hand now and leading me down the block. I turned around to see if the others were watching. They were. They were all just standing there. All except for Jeffrey. He was starting to follow us. The guy didn't seem to know when to give it up.

Kelsey led me to a pawnshop called Honest

John's. Inside, the place was crammed with all kinds of music gear. Gretsch and Fender guitars were hanging from the walls. Amps were stacked up on the floor and a couple of dismantled drum sets were scattered around. Behind the glass counter was a bald guy with a hearing aid.

"John, this is my friend, Cody."

John looked up and smiled. "It's good to see you, Kelsey. How are things at home?"

"They've been worse," she answered. "What about you? How's business?"

"Always the same," John answered, putting a finger to his ear to adjust the volume on his hearing aid.

The little bell rang as the door opened again. I turned around to discover Jeffrey had followed us here. I shook my head in disbelief.

John smiled at Jeffrey. He swept his hand around the roomful of musical chaos. "Look around, kids," he said. "It's all for sale. Try out anything that looks interesting." Then he turned away and fiddled with a pile of cameras on the counter.

That's when I began to realize I'd been tricked. Jeffrey had picked up a Fender Stratocaster and plugged it into an amp. He hit a couple of chords, tuned a string, and then cranked up the overdrive on the amp. I walked away towards the back of the store, pretending I wasn't interested. I didn't realize anyone into rap could play a musical instrument. Especially not Jeffrey.

I tried to ignore him. I tried to ignore both of

them. But Kelsey had plugged an old Yamaha keyboard into another amp and was hitting some chords.

Now I was beginning to get the picture. "No way!" I shouted at her. "Not in a million years."

Kelsey pretended she didn't hear me. I looked at John. He didn't seem to be paying attention to any of us, despite the noise. I wanted out of there.

I walked past Kelsey and Jeffrey just as they were starting to get in sync. As I was walking out the door, Kelsey started to sing. I immediately recognized the song. Even without a mic, her voice came on powerful and full of impact. She was singing "Daredevil Difference," the first song of hers I ever heard, the first one I had jammed on when Scream Static was beginning to exist.

I stood there, outside the pawnshop, staring at the cars going by in the afternoon sun. I stood there listening to her voice. And then the guitar lead came on strong. Man, she was a shrewd one. Was this whole scene really a setup?

Jeffrey's guitar came up loud and wailing. It blasted out of the pawnshop onto the street. Backed by the keyboard chords, it gave a wild, haunting shriek that stabbed like an ice pick into my brain. I wanted to turn and walk away but I didn't move. The guitar notes zapped like lightning through my skull, reminding me of the not-so-old but dead-and-gone days of SS. It was a hard, powerful, and overwhelming sound that flowed out onto the street. It was full of pride and hurt and outrage and courage and anger all at once.

When Kelsey started singing again, there was some perfect melting of voice and shrill overdrive guitar that just about made my socks crawl down into my shoes.

Suddenly from my right, some old geezer came storming out of the drugstore and pushed past me into Honest John's. I turned around and saw him screaming something at Jeffrey, then screaming at John. But John must have hosted his share of music talent in his store before. So when the drugstore dude started screaming, "No more noise, John. No more of this horrible noise!" John just smiled and went back to his cameras on the counter.

The man was still screaming, "No more noise!" when I walked back in there. There was a selection of drumsticks on the counter. I picked out a pair, looked for something handy to bash. The drum parts were scattered and I didn't see anything easy to get at. But there was a big plastic trash can by the door. I had to move the music critic out of the way to get to it. Then I turned it over and I started to play. Kelsey did another verse. Jeffrey took the cue for an extended lead riff and eventually the drugstore guy couldn't stand it any more. He retreated back to his store.

When the tune was over, I turned the trash can upright and set the sticks back on the counter.

Kelsey and Jeffrey had a look on them like they had just finished a sold-out performance at the Metro Centre. But then Jeffrey set the guitar down, turned off the amp, and cleared his throat. "Well, I guess I gotta get moving," he said, trying to sound really nonchalant. "Anybody got the time?"

"Yeah, man," I said, undoing the watch from my wrist and handing it to him. "I got the time. Here you go."

Chapter 17

We hadn't been practising for more than a month when Barry told us there was a gig coming up that we couldn't turn down. "There's going to be this rally on Gottingen Street," he said. "Kind of like a big block party to bring people together and make a stand against violence in the city. It's being put together by a whole bunch of community groups."

"You must be joking," I said.

Barry shook his head. "You rather we party with the PFMM?"

I held my drumsticks in the air. "Hey, I wasn't complaining. A gig's a gig. I just wanted to make sure I knew who I was working for."

I looked at Jeffrey. The guy was actually laughing. We were getting along pretty good, considering our past history. It worried me sometimes that I didn't hate him like I used to. But I tried not to let it get to me. We played music. The three of us were good. Scream Static had just gone a little weirder, that's all.

"It's getting worse, isn't it?" Kelsey asked Barry.

"What do you mean?"

"More beatings," she said, looking very serious all of a sudden. "Little kids getting punched around at school. Kids on the street getting swarmed. More fights between black and white gangs. Is it just 'cause I'm paying attention or is it something else?"

Kelsey was in very serious mood. The girl actually sat around thinking about this stuff. She probably guessed that I sometimes missed being part of the downtown action. I really felt like bashing someone once in a while. Even music couldn't use up all my energy.

So here we were — three people with problems who had become a loud and angry band with something to sing about. Jeffrey had never really fit in anywhere. Kelsey had been at odds with the world since the day she was born. And I don't exactly know how to describe my problem. It seemed I was always really ticked off about something.

"Yeah," Barry said. "It's worse. You see it in the news. You see it on the street. Women are afraid to go out at night. Parents are afraid to let their kids walk down the street. You got white kids picking on black kids. Blacks picking on whites. Men stalking women. Gay bashing."

"Hey, don't sweat it. It's just the way things are," I told him.

Barry pretended he didn't hear me. "So what's

the story? Are we in or out? You guys want the gig or not?"

"How much we getting paid?" I asked. I was a pro, right? I should know how much it was worth.

"The place will be crawling with media people. We're talking about twenty thousand dollars worth of free publicity here," Barry said.

"In other words, we don't get paid, Cody," Jeffrey said.

"That's fine with me," Kelsey said. "I think the whole capitalist thing sucks anyway. We don't need the money."

Now Kelsey was putting down money. Every day it was a new twist with her. It was hard to keep my head adjusted to it.

"I bet that if we don't do this gig, they got no one, right?"

"Wrong," Barry said. "Prime Targets is interested if you guys aren't ready to do it." Prime Targets was Alex's new band, the one managed by Giles, the band so clean they were being groomed for big success. "Okay, we'll do it," I conceded. I knew it was a lost cause from the beginning. "Who could turn down twenty thousand dollars worth of free publicity?"

For the big event they closed off a couple of blocks of Gottingen. It had a pretty cool feel to it with no cars, just people filling the street. We had our gear set up on the back of a flatbed trailer that acted as a stage and Barry borrowed a serious sound system for the event.

Around the perimeter of the crowd were cops. I'd never seen so many police in one place, but I'd given up worrying every time I saw a cop. If they wanted me, they would have hauled me in long ago. Besides, sometimes I convinced myself I was a changed person. Today I was on the side of the good guys. Maybe the cops didn't trust the organizers of this thing. Maybe they didn't trust the crowd. With this many people on the street in this part of town, anything could happen.

Before we could play, we had to listen to a bunch of speeches by some people who thought they could fix all the problems of the city by just standing up and talking them all away. The first one to take the mic was this skinny old feminist name Maude. She was a bit much for me to handle. Next, a black minister gave a little preachy thing about standing up to injustice. He reminded me of somebody I'd seen in a rap video. The audience was this really crazy mix of black and white people, street life and university types, mothers with little kids, suburbanites and high school kids from all over town. The whole time the speakers were hogging the mics, I kept thinking that this was going to be one very tough audience.

The crowd was so big, I couldn't see the back of it. I kept looking at the faces and trying to figure what sort of music each one listened to. Man, we didn't have anything for any of them. All we had was our stuff — it was new, it was raw, and it was loud. Thinking about it made me nervous.

I saw Jeffrey talking to some of his old street friends. A few of them gave me the creeps. Suddenly I felt somebody squeeze my hand. It was Kelsey. She was smiling at me. She'd been real intent on listening to the speakers but now she was paying attention to me. "I'm really glad we're doing this," she told me. "I'm glad we're doing this together."

"Me too," I said. "We'll blow them all away."

Another speaker came up to the podium, somebody who said he was from the Halifax Peace Society. I wasn't paying too much attention to him. In fact, I was thinking about Kelsey. I felt like that invisible barrier between us had finally broken down. I wanted to tell her that. I wanted to tell her how I really felt about her — not just how much I respected her music but how much I cared for her. But I knew as soon as I opened my mouth I would sound like an idiot.

Just then, Alex arrived on the scene with some of his band. He walked right up to us, dressed in clothes that must have cost a couple hundred bucks.

"Hi Slick," Kelsey said. "Good to see you." She didn't hold any grudges. I couldn't be that polite.

"I'm glad you guys are doing this show," Alex said. "It's your style."

"What do you mean?" I asked. I could detect a put-down when I heard it.

"They asked us first," Alex said. "But Giles thought it was a little too sensitive so we turned them down."

I got the picture loud and clear. But I didn't believe him, the little snot.

"Besides, we've got a plane to catch later this afternoon. It's our first really big gig."

"Congratulations," Kelsey told Alex, pretending she really cared. Kelsey was squeezing my hand harder. She knew it might look bad for me to punch the guy's lights out or rip his tongue out of his mouth, right there in front of everybody at the anti-violence rally.

"Yeah, congratulations," I told Alex.

"How's the new guitar player working out?" Alex asked, pointing over at Jeffrey. One of his other band buddies beside him was whispering something and all three of them were cracking up.

"You know how it is breaking in a new musician," Kelsey said, sounding very professional. "It's tough at first and then things click."

I couldn't wait until Alex heard just how good his replacement was. But I wasn't going to say what was on my mind. I just said, "You'll have to excuse us. We gotta get ready to do some music."

The speeches were winding down. We pulled Jeffrey away from his friends and walked back behind the flatbed trailer stage.

"Do you really think they asked Alex's band first?" I asked Kelsey.

"It doesn't matter," Jeffrey said.

"But I wanna know," I said. Up until then I had been hanging onto my confidence. Now it was slipping down to my knees.

The final speaker was finishing up and I knew we were about to be introduced. Why was it so important to me whether we were asked first or not?

"I don't know," Kelsey answered. "I honestly don't. But it doesn't matter. We've been wanting an audience for a long time. Now we've got it. And it's a big one. You think I'm not nervous too?"

Whoa. She had come out and said it. She had read me like a book. That's what I was feeling. I was just looking for excuses but the truth was I wasn't just nervous. I was shaking-in-my-boots scared. I'd never felt like this before. This was completely different. I didn't know if I could go on.

I listened to the lady on the stage introducing us. "And now a band that shares our concerns for making these streets safe. You know them for their underground hits like 'The Condom Song' and 'Daredevil Difference.' Here they are — Scream Static!"

My knees felt like jelly and my arms like rubber as I walked out onto the stage and sat down at the drums. In front of us was a sea of faces. People were clapping and cheering but the crowd scared me. I felt like they were all my enemies. I knew it was up to me to get the beat going, to start hammering and get the music moving. I couldn't see whether Jeffrey was scared or not because he had his back to me. But I caught the look on Kelsey's face. It told me she felt the same way I did.

The clapping had subsided. People were waiting for something to happen. For a split second I felt frozen, immobile. What if I really messed this up for good? said that voice of doubt inside my head. I closed my eyes and tried to pretend I was back in Kelsey's garage. It wasn't working.

But then I heard one single note coming from Kelsey's keyboard. She was holding down one key. The sound of that one note was like electricity connecting us. It was like some powerful, insistent force recharging all the batteries of my will. Jeffrey joined in now with the first thunderous chord of "Downtown Dangerous" and I felt the energy double. I felt the connection between all three of us and suddenly my arms were moving. My eyes were still closed, my head tilted up to the sky, but I was in motion. I was letting the rhythm of my drums take over as we launched into the intro for the song.

With the monster PA system it sounded like an avalanche of sound. I heard each drumbeat echo off the walls of the storefronts. I opened my eyes as Kelsey began to sing the first verse and I saw the sea of faces again. But this time it wasn't like they were my enemies. They were all my friends.

We roared, we wailed, we made music that must have shaken the foundations of the buildings. Kelsey's voice was strong and her songs were angry. Her anger was an anger of caring. I listened to her words again and knew for sure the organizers had asked us first. Kelsey's songs were right in sync with this anti-violence thing. We were now the centre of all that energy. As I watched Jeffrey launch into space with his magnificent lead guitar work, the irony of the moment came back to haunt me. And when I looked past him out into the crowd, I saw Alex watching, knowing we'd replaced him with someone better. That made me feel good. I knew I really didn't care how different Jeffrey was. I didn't care if he was a Martian with three heads. He was in the band and he was one of us.

There were other faces now in the crowd that I recognized, other faces I wish I had never known. Jordan, Logan, and Eric were bullying their way from the outside fringe right up towards the stage.

They looked out of place here — these three ugly goons with black leather jackets, metal-toed workboots, and monster bad attitudes — Eric with his newly shaved head, Logan with his creepy sunglasses, and Jordan with the hate screaming out from his face. Just looking at them made me realize how different I was from what I'd been. But then I realized something was different about them as well. They were here in broad daylight. They weren't just sneaking away from some crime in the night. They had come down here for a purpose and it wasn't for the music.

Chapter 18

After about forty-five minutes, we took our break as planned. I had a kind of glow on from the thrill of the clapping and cheering from the crowd. SS had finally and truly gone public and we were a hit.

I came down from the stage with my head buzzing to find my old buddies waiting for me. "We gotta talk," Jordan said to me, never sounding more polite or friendly, though his face said something different. I could tell he'd been drinking, which meant Logan and Eric had been as well. Who knows what else they'd been doing.

"I don't think I want to talk right now."

"Don't worry," Logan said. "It's cool. We just have some news we wanted to share. Good news."

So I followed them to the end of the trailer and away from the stage. We sat down on some crates. Kelsey watched us. She looked worried and with good reason.

"I can't believe you got a loser like that playing guitar with you," Eric said, rubbing his hand across his bald head.

"He's good, isn't he?" I said.

Eric sucked in his breath and shook his head. I think they were testing me. With their own perverse sense of loyalty, I think they wanted to believe that deep down I was still one of them.

"You remember how you used to say that we should do some real damage to that Lebanese store?" Jordan said.

"I remember."

"Foreigners come over here stealing all the jobs, man," Logan said. "It's not right."

Logan had never even tried to get a job, even a part-time one. And I don't even think his old man had done a day's work or ever wanted to.

"Gotta show 'em a lesson, right?" Jordan pointed out.

"So we kicked in the window the other night. Stole some smokes and papers and stuff. You shoulda been there."

Eric pulled out his wallet. He pulled out a fistful of bills. "And look at this. Ripped it off some Paki kid in Clayton Park last night."

"Like taking candy from a baby." Logan was all smiles behind his shades.

"Point is, Cody, you're missing out on all the fun. And we feel sorta bad. We've been through a lot together. We thought we should give you another chance." Jordan was serious. I think he actually did feel sorry for me. Or maybe he had chosen to ignore Kelsey's song lyrics and liked the idea of having an up-and-coming musician as part of his crowd. Their idea of fun, though, now sounded stupid and cruel to me.

"She got to you, didn't she?" Jordan asked.

Yeah, I wanted to say. She did get to me. The music got to me. I was different now. There was no going back. But this wasn't the time for lectures.

"You guys are too much," I said smiling. "But I'm really glad you came to hear the music."

I left them with their jaws unhinged and walked back to the stage.

I felt much cooler, much more together when I sat back down at my drums for the second set. Meeting with my old boys didn't even faze me.

I looked over my shoulder to see what they would do next. A couple of cops were talking to them. It looked like they were hassling Jordan.

"Ready?" Kelsey asked me.

"No," I said. I nodded towards my old friends. They were surrounded by six cops in total now. They were being led out front, out through the crowd and away from the stage. People pulled back as they were led through. I didn't understand it. We had just been talking. I knew they hadn't done anything wrong. Not today anyway. I watched as one cop grabbed for Jordan's shoulder and pushed him along. Jordan tried to jerk away from him and Eric reached over to take the cop's hand off Jordan.

When I saw two of the cops pull out their clubs, I had to react. This was all wrong. I knew exactly why Jordan, Eric, and Logan were being hassled right now. It wasn't anything they had done. It was because they looked bad, they looked tough and they looked like they might cause trouble.

But no one had a right to kick somebody out of here just because of the way they looked.

I jumped down from the stage and made my way through the crowd to where the action was.

Maybe because I was part of the band the police couldn't just ignore me when I demanded, "Why are you pushing them around? They have a right to be here."

Three cops now had clubs in their hands. They looked good and ready to use them. Another officer was eyeing me. I had this weird feeling they knew who we were . . . they knew what we had all done.

"Get those creeps out of here," someone in the crowd yelled. "They're troublemakers. They have no right to be here!"

The absurdity of that idiot shouting these words hit me like slap in the face. Why weren't Jordan, Eric, and Logan allowed to be here at this rally? Why should they have to leave? Was this event only for the privileged who looked normal?

"These are my friends," I said to the police. "I invited them backstage. I want them to stay."

I knew it was a gamble. I knew the cops had good reason to worry about these three being here. But they were here and that was something. Maybe one of Kelsey's songs would get to them. Maybe something about these people getting together to say "no more violence" would mean something. But if they were booted out of here now . . . well, I know exactly how I would feel. I'd be madder than before.

"Sorry, son," one of the officers said to me. "These guys are trouble." They began to push them away.

Jordan had the look on his face, the look that said he'd let someone, even a cop, push him only so far.

Kelsey and Jeffrey had followed me off the stage. They were beside me now. Everybody in the crowd knew something was going on.

"Let them stay!" Kelsey shouted at the cops. But they weren't listening. More police were moving in now. What they saw was a flashpoint, some serious trouble about to break out.

"Come on, man," Jeffrey said, grabbing onto the sleeve of one of the uniforms. "You don't have to kick them out of here."

I don't think the cop got a good look at Jeffrey. He just knew someone had grabbed him and he wasn't going to wait and see what happened next. He turned and swung his club. Jeffrey saw it coming. He was quick. He ducked out of the way but ended up falling on the ground.

"No!" screamed Kelsey.

Eric and Jordan used the distraction to try to

get away. The cops were trying to hold onto them. Logan was down on the ground covering his head like he expected to get it next. Some of Jeffrey's friends were pushing through the crowd coming to help him. They started to push the cops away from Jeffrey and the police were pushing back. People were shoving, everybody was starting to freak, and I knew in a few seconds someone was going to get hurt.

I quickly backed away and jumped up on stage. I grabbed the mic from the stand and looked over to Barry at the soundboard. Gave him a thumb in the air. He knew I wanted the volume fully cranked.

"Okay," I said breathlessly into the mic, making maybe the first speech I ever made in my life. "Everybody be cool." The words reverberated off the buildings. "Just everybody be cool."

I guess I was loud enough to make everyone at least take notice. I had their attention now. I looked over towards the disturbance. Eric and Jordan had their arms twisted up behind them. A couple of Jeffrey's friends were squared off in front of two cops with clubs. Logan was still somewhere down on the ground, I guessed, cowering. And Kelsey was right there in the middle of it. If I couldn't say the right thing, somebody would get hurt. Maybe just a face in the crowd or maybe it would be Kelsey.

"It's all a misunderstanding," I said. I was looking at the cops but I was talking to everyone. "It's not right to throw my friends out of here. They came here like everybody else did and they have a right to be here. They're being picked on because they look like they don't fit in."

The crowd was almost quiet, but people were all jammed up around the police. People were taking sides.

"Everybody just back off," I said. "Yeah, just back off, okay?"

"How about it?" I said, looking at the cops, then around at the crowd. "Back off. Please."

I saw one of the cops looking at me. He turned to the others, nodded. They backed off. Logan got up off the ground. Eric, Jordan, and Logan were now standing there with everybody watching them. That was the moment I knew I had made the biggest gamble of my life. Maybe Jordan would bust someone. Maybe Logan would think it was a great chance to turn the whole scene into a riot. Or maybe Eric would spit at one of the cops and then run for it.

Instead, someone else in the crowd yelled out, "Let 'em stay!"

"Yeah, that's right," someone else shouted. "Let everyone stay. This is our party, right? And everyone's invited."

A few people clapped and cheered but a lot of people were just plain confused. When things got quiet, I saw Jeffrey and Kelsey coming back up to the stage. Somebody helped both of them hop up onto the front.

I caught a glimpse of Jordan. I saw that old

familiar hate on his face. He put his hands to his mouth and shouted something at me — something loud, angry, and full of the same old hate. "Forget it, Cody. We don't want to stay. You can all go to hell as far as I'm concerned."

But no one shouted back anything at them. I watched as Eric, Logan, and Jordan weaved towards the back of the crowd and found their way out of there on their own. The cops let them be.

Kelsey was holding down a minor chord on the keyboard. I felt a twinge of loss as I stumbled back to my drum set, tripping over one of the power cords. I wondered if we had just won or lost a battle. I wondered if any of this had meant anything at all.

Kelsey launched us into "Daredevil Difference" and it all came back to me — the early days. The way I used to be. I knew I could never go back, I knew I had changed and I was hoping that sooner or later something good would happen for Logan, Jordan, and Eric, and then they would change too. Maybe. That's what I hoped for as I sat there and played my heart out on my drums in front of those people on Gottingen Street in Halifax.

After the concert, I felt oddly at home among this crowd. Everybody kept telling us what a wonderful set we played. Jeffrey introduced me to a couple of his friends. I acted like it was no big deal even though I still felt really uncomfortable and wouldn't let them get too friendly.

Kelsey introduced me to the old grey-haired

woman who had given one of the speeches. "Cody, this is Maude."

I nodded. "Hi," I said.

"You're a good man, Cody," she said. "I admire you for what you did. And I like your music too."

Oh, right, like I really believed her. But Kelsey was watching me. It was another one of her tests. I wanted to pass this one. I truly did.

I pointed my drumsticks straight at the woman, "The way I figure it, lady, it goes like this. We're all different in some way or another. And it really doesn't matter. We just gotta do what we gotta do and learn to live with everybody else."

She gave me a hug just then and I was caught off guard. She was old and she was skinny and I felt her thin, bony arms pulled tight around me with a kind of strength that shocked me. When she let me go, she playfully hit me hard on the arm with her knuckle. "Keep it up," she told me, then turned and walked away.

Jeffrey's friends were laughing at me. I guess I looked pretty bewildered. That's when Kelsey slipped an arm around me and said, "I think it went pretty well."

"Yeah," I said. "Twenty thousand dollars worth of free publicity. I think we scored big." But I knew what she meant. I just didn't have the words in me right then to tell her what I had finally figured out.

"Let's go find something to eat. I'm starving," she said.

"Me too. But I'm broke."

"I'm buying," Kelsey said. "Let's stash the gear in the garage and then I'll take you out to dinner."

"This isn't like a date or anything?" I asked.

"No way," she said, the sweet smile on her face telling me the opposite. "You think I'd go out on a date with a big ugly thug like you?"

And I knew then that it was the beginning of something very fine. My life, for the first time in a long while, was looking pretty damn good.

Afterword

Violence in any form sucks. Once, when I was a kid, I had my head bashed into the windscreen of a car until blood ran down my face. I had just finished playing a gig with a band named Prodigy at a Friday night dance. I had tried to stop one guy from punching out the lights of another guy who had said the wrong thing at the wrong time. As a result, I got hammered by someone who had obviously spent a lot more time practising with his fists than I had.

This novel is about music but it is also about violence. You might wonder, why is this guy who is opposed to violence writing a book where the main character is a bully and a thug who gets his jollies by bashing anyone he sees as "different"? Isn't there already too much violence in the movies and on TV and even in books?

The answer is yes and no.

Yes, most of the violence you see in the media is there for shock and entertainment value. And it still sucks. There's no doubt in my mind that it helps to increase violence in the real world. The reason I explored violence in this book is because I was interested in examining the root of violence both in myself and in the world around me. That's what this story is all about.

It was a rough book to write. Cody was a difficult character for me to get into. In order to write a good novel, to some degree I have to become the character who is telling the story. So imagine for a minute what happens when this author becomes Cody.

Several times in my life, I've actively been involved in protests and other activities to stop wars, to get rid of nuclear weapons, to promote gun control, to reduce violence on TV, and to counter racial hatred. If you read any of my other books, you'll find that there's a strong underlying theme of "tolerance." Everyone should get along with everyone else no matter how different they are. I'm a pacifist, too, which means that I think all forms of fighting — schoolyard and battleground— are stupid. I'll do what I can to end violence.

So figure this: somewhere inside of the complex of personalities that is me, Cody exists. I think there's a little bit of Cody in you as well, no matter how freaky that sounds.

Intolerant tough guys hate others — immigrants, gays, racial minorities, emo kids, or rappers — because of basic insecurities, frustration, and an anger that grows from a very primary fear. We all share some of that insecurity and the fear that goes along with it. Most people don't act out the violence that results from it, but some do.

Having written from Cody's point of view, I think I understand the problem a little bit better. If Cody remained the same stubborn, pigheaded bully that he was at the beginning of this chain of events, there would have been no story here. Fiction, though, is created around characters and the changes they go through. Cody is a different drummer by the end of the book and therein lies the tale.

But I wasn't writing a book exclusively about violence. I was also writing a book about music. The same night that I had my head bashed in while trying to stop a fight, I had just had a great session playing lead guitar in my band in front of a crowd of a couple hundred kids. We had played our hearts out. We wailed and thrashed and sang and stomped and jammed away until everybody's ears rang and neighbours were complaining that we were disturbing the peace. But when we had to stop at the end of the gig, we knew we had succeeded in making the music work through our drums, guitars, and keyboard, and through us as well. Maybe that's why I had felt invincible and had to be brought back to cold, hard reality by a guy who did his communicating with fists instead of guitar picks.

I like to think that I haven't lost the music. I still play guitar. I've recently recorded some more new tunes adapting my poetry to music. You can search for the music videos of Lesley Choyce and the SurfPoets on YouTube or on my website, lesleychoyce.com. So, when Kelsey, Cody, and Alex work out a new tune, I'm there with them at the heart of the musical creative process.

The music and the message that Cody and Kelsey create is inextricably entwined. The songs have sound but they also have lyrics with real content. As sometimes happens with books, original music with real lyric content is often the first to get condemned, to get censored, to get banned. Maybe someone will even want to attack this novel for its violence, for its language, or because Cody is not a respectable character. Maybe it should be kept out of the schools because it deals with sensitive subjects.

If that were to happen, I think that we'd all be losing something. We'd be losing a chance to openly discuss the root problems of violence. We'd be giving over the power of influence to TV and movie producers who glorify the death and destruction that has become so much a part of our lives. Novels provide a fictional world to examine our deepest concerns. It's my hope that this novel will help readers take a look at their own neighbourhoods and think about ways to reduce hostility and intolerance in whatever form it takes.

Lesley Choyce
Lawrencetown Beach, Nova Scotia

Read more great teen fiction from SideStreets.

Ask for them at your local library, bookstore, or order them online at www.lorimer.ca.

Hell's Hotel
by Lesley Choyce

Tara thought she could handle anything, but now her life is falling apart. Maybe she's not so different from her friend Jenn, a homeless teen, after all. Running away seems like the only option for Tara, until the night she spends in an abandoned building that kids on the street call Hell's Hotel.

ISBN: 978-1-55277-022-1 (paperback)

Last Chance
by Lesley Choyce

Melanie and Trent can't live at home, and they can't rely on the social support system. Even working at part time jobs they barely make enough to stay off the streets and stay in school. Trent knows of a way out — but the cost is high.

ISBN: 978-1-55277-444-1 (paperback)

New Blood
by Peter McPhee

After a gang of thugs beat him up, Callum's parents decide to move. But the problems don't end for Callum in their new town. Callum's deep inner scars make school a continuous battleground.

ISBN: 978-1-55028-996-1 (paperback)

Final Takedown
by Brent R. Sherrard

The judge has given Elias a warning: Shape up, or do time in juvie. But how's a guy to keep out of trouble when his mom's an alchie, he's kicked out of school, and his best friend wants him to join in on a takedown that he knows isn't going to work?

ISBN: 978-1-55277-523-3 (paperback)

Wasted
by Brent R. Sherrard

Jacob likes to party, but, unlike his alcoholic father, he knows that he can easily overcome his drug and alcohol abuse. When when a terrible tragedy takes Jacob to the breaking point, he discovers just how powerful dependency can be.

ISBN: 978-1-55277-419-9 (paperback)

Scab
by Robert Rayner

Julian Faye, aka Scab, knows all about being picked on. For years he's been bullied by his classmates and neglected by his parents. Now, seventeen and a gifted photographer, he's faced with a dilemma: Get the shot that'll launch his career, or save the only person who's ever given a damn about him.

ISBN: 978-1-55277-482-3 (paperback)

Out
by Sandra Diersch
No one in Alex's world is who they seem to be. Alex struggles with his faith when he witnesses a church member cheating on his wife and learns that his brother is gay. When his brother is brutally attacked, Alex is forced to decide where his loyalties lie and what he really believes in.
ISBN: 978-1-55277-421-2 (paperback)

War Games
by Jacqueline Guest
Ryan's father is on his first tour of duty in Afghanistan, and Ryan is thrilled. He'll finally get a break from his overbearing father and be able to spend more time off the military base. But Ryan soon becomes entangled in a world of deceit, which forces him to come to terms with the extreme risks his father is facing overseas.
ISBN: 978-1-55277-035-1 (paperback)

All In
by Monique Polak
Todd's never been much of a student, but he's got plenty of street smarts and he's a mean poker player. Todd's always had a thing for Claire, the most beautiful girl in school, but Claire likes nice things. If Todd wants to date her, he'll need cash, and plenty of it. Soon, a weekly poker game turns into a costly and dangerous obsession, and Todd's luck begins to change.
ISBN: 978-1-55028-912-1 (paperback)

LORIMER